Wild With You

Also by Sara Jane Stone

Hero By Night
Caught in the Act
Full Exposure

Search and Seduce
Command Control
Command Performance

Wild With You

Book Four:
Independence Falls

SARA JANE STONE

AVONIMPULSE
An Imprint of HarperCollinsPublishers

Excerpt from *Changing Everything* copyright © 2015 by Molly McAdams.

Excerpt from *Chase Me* copyright © 2015 by Tessa Bailey.

Excerpt from *Yours to Hold* copyright © 2015 by Darcy Burke.

Excerpt from *The Elusive Lord Everhart* copyright © 2015 by Vivienne Lorret.

EPub Edition APRIL 2015 ISBN: 9780062389183
Print Edition ISBN: 9780062389145

10 9 8 7 6 5 4 3 2 1

Acknowledgments

THANK YOU TO all of the wonderful readers who have fallen in love with the Independence Falls series! I love reading your e-mails, messages, and comments on Facebook. Every time a reader tells me how much they love these characters, their words brighten my day. And to everyone who posted pictures and suggestions for Georgia's wedding gown on Facebook, I hope you like the one I selected!

My stories are a team effort. Without my agent Jill Marsal, and my talented editor Amanda Bergeron, *Wild With You* would be a very different book. I'm so thankful for their insights.

Thank you to my publicity team, Maria Silva at Avon Books and Kelley at Smut Book Junkies. And to all of the bloggers who promote and review my stories—I am so grateful for all that you do!

I also want to give a shout-out to my fellow authors

who have supported my writing, and this series in particular. Maya Rodale, I don't know if I would ever survive a writer's conference without you. Samanthe Beck and Toni Blake, thank you for the awesome quotes for my books, and for keeping me up half the night reading your stories. Lauren Blakely, Laura Kaye, Darcy Burke, and Tawny Weber, thank you for the social media love. And to all of the Avon Impulse authors, you guys are such a talented, supportive group!

Happy Reading!

Sara Jane Stone

THE BLACK SUITCASE with the gold designer label came out of nowhere, knocking Brody Summers on his ass outside the Portland airport hotel. He looked up, planning to growl at the person wielding the bag, and saw legs. Long, shapely legs designed to lead a man's thoughts straight to the bedroom. And those shoes—heck, her black and gold high heels matched her suitcase.

His gaze traveled north taking in every inch of smooth skin. Two questions flashed through his mind.

What would she look like bound to his bed? And: *Where were her pants?*

Her heels clicked on the pavement as she stepped closer. He caught a glimpse of her short skirt, peeking out between the tails of her long top. The black button-down collared shirt mixed business and pleasure in a way that sent his imagination on a side trip, wondering what she wore beneath the silky, form-fitting material.

Probably a matching bra and panty set that cost too much to rip off her petite curved body without inviting tears. The woman who'd knocked him flat on his ass looked about as expensive as her luggage.

And she was groomed to perfection. Her long blond hair fell in waves around her shoulders and her red lips quirked up.

"Lost your footing, cowboy?" Her voice possessed a low, throaty quality designed for whispering naughty pleas after the fancy clothes hit the floor.

But cowboy? What the heck? Brody raised his hand and touched his head. Nope, his Moore Timber baseball cap still covered his dirty brown hair.

"Your shoes." She pointed to the shiny black cowboy boots he'd dug out of the back of his truck. His work boots needed to dry out after trampling across the wet, muddy mountainside. "Need a hand getting up?" she added, extending one perfectly manicured hand.

"Thank you, ma'am, but I can manage." He pushed off the ground. Standing in front of her, he realized she wasn't as tall as she'd appeared from the ground. At six-foot-three plus the cowboy boots, he towered over her.

"Ma'am," she murmured, her green eyes shining with amusement. "I forgot how formal you are out here."

"Returning home?" While she looked him over, he eyed the automatic door behind her, which led to the hotel lobby. He wasn't shy. Not by a long shot. But compared to her, Brody knew he looked like he'd spent the day rolling in dirt.

"I'm here for work, but this isn't my first time in Oregon." She extended her hand again. "I'm Kat."

Knowing it would be rude to refuse, he shook her hand. "Brody."

Her eyes widened for a second and he drew away from her firm grip, guessing his callused palm had caught her by surprise. A woman who matched her fancy shoes to her luggage was probably accustomed to well-groomed men in suits.

"I believe I owe you a drink, Brody. For knocking you to the ground."

After spending the past twelve hours combing Hood Mountain for a lost family, he was overdue for a beer. But first he needed to get cleaned up. "Thanks, but I have a date with the shower."

Kat's eyes narrowed, her gaze sharpening as if he'd issued a challenge when he said "shower." While the thought of inviting this near stranger to join him appealed to the same part of his anatomy that appreciated the heck out of her short skirt, high heels, and sexy top, he steered clear of one-night territory with women he'd just met. And he didn't plan on making an exception tonight.

Duty had landed him in Portland and he needed to stay focused on his missions. Somewhere on the snow-capped mountain, a ten-year-old boy was wandering around looking for the parents Brody and his team had located earlier. Heck, if he'd had his way, he'd still be out there searching for the kid. But the team leader had or-

dered him, and the rest of the guys who'd been working for twelve hours, to take a break. He hated walking
away without finishing the job, but he had to admit that
a fresh team of search-and-rescue volunteers might cover
more ground. And Brody had been bone-tired from the
moment he started the search, thanks to the "mission"
waiting for him back home.

His family.

Back home, his little brother sank deeper into depression as the hope of recovering the short-term memory
he'd lost to a logging accident dimmed. Sure, Josh was
lucky to be alive after getting hit in the head with a metal
hook. He'd spent weeks in a coma following the accident.
But writing down every detail about his day-to-day life
drove Josh crazy.

Now, thanks to the doctor who'd agreed to include his
brother in her clinical trial, Josh had a fighting chance.
Brody planned to meet Dr. Westbury, the famous neurologist, here in the morning and drive her back to Independence Falls. Before that he needed a solid six, maybe
seven hours of sleep, not a detour into casual sex.

"Nice meeting you, Kat." He moved around her, heading for the double doors. Now, when he'd finally found
someone who might be able to help his little brother, was
not the time to find out how Little Miss Perfect would
look in his shower.

"Brody."

He paused by the open doorway and glanced over his
shoulder.

"If you change your mind," she said, one hand clutching the handle of the designer bag that moonlighted as a weapon. "Come find me in the hotel bar."

"I'll do that." He suspected his ironclad willpower would keep him in his room. But looking back at her, Brody had to admit he wanted a taste of perfection.

Chapter 2

KAT FROZE ON the edge of the generic carpet separating the hotel's attempt at a fine-dining restaurant and lounge from the lobby. The boy she'd been half in love with throughout high school sat at the black granite bar with one hand wrapped around a pint glass and the other clutching his cell phone. Only he wasn't a teenager anymore. Brody Summers was a prime example of droolworthy male perfection.

And it looked like he'd changed his mind about meeting her for a drink.

Excitement threatened her usually logical mind. Brody Summers was sitting at the bar, waiting for *her*.

Earlier, when she'd glanced down at the pavement, her first thought was: I took out Brody Summers with my suitcase! But fate rarely worked in her favor. And it had certainly never dropped a hot-as-sin man at her feet. In the moment, she'd assumed the lingering effects of her Brody Summers's infatuation had blurred her vision.

Those deep brown eyes had haunted her dreams in high school, and later, during her long years in medical school, her fantasies. Add those broad shoulders and the muscular, imposing body, and the grown-up version was oh-so worth it. Then he'd said his name, confirming that he was in fact her crush from the town she'd sworn up and down she'd never set foot in again—Independence Falls.

But Brody hadn't recognized her.

Not that she blamed him. There were days when she could barely connect the painfully shy foster kid who'd grown up wearing whatever the charity bin had to offer with the person she saw in the mirror. After she'd left Independence Falls, Kat had traded her hand-me-downs for designer labels. And she'd changed her mousy brown hair to an eye-catching blond.

Still, he was here now. Sitting at the bar, waiting for her.

A healthy dose of reality caught hold of her runaway hopes, anchoring the would-be fantasy. He was here because she'd caught his attention on the sidewalk. He'd looked at her legs as if he wanted to strip away her skirt and explore. But looking didn't always lead to action. And it wasn't as if he harbored an ancient crush that was pushing him to seize the moment.

Brody Summers probably didn't remember the shy sophomore he'd stumbled upon in the Independence Falls High art room Super Gluing her shoes back together.

Or the fact that he'd stayed to help, talking to her as if he gave a damn about her sneakers. And not once had he suggested that she ditch her worn, ripped shoes and get new ones. It was as if he understood the sacrifices that came with poverty. Or maybe he believed it when she'd told him these were her lucky shoes. He didn't know her well enough to realize that luck had abandoned her at age six and never looked back.

Until now.

Maybe.

She'd caught his attention again. And this time Brody Summers hadn't looked at her with pity brewing in his eyes while he saved her sneakers. If she'd known knocking him over would get his attention, she would have tried it in high school. Maybe in the weeks and months following the Super Glue adventure, when she'd looked at him from afar waiting and hoping for him to notice her.

Oh, he'd never been rude. Brody had nodded and smiled, waving when they passed in the halls. But he'd never looked at her as if he was picturing her in his shower.

Because knocking him over and winning an I-want-you look only worked when Dr. Katherine Arnold plowed into him with a bag that cost more than the sum total of her worldly possessions back when she was a teenager. From her designer luggage to her perfect blond hair, she presented a very different picture now. And it had been a long time since anyone had offered her pity.

But in high school?

From the moment she'd walked through the doors

of Independence Falls High in her freshman year, the other kids had left her alone as if her condition was contagious. Halfway through her first semester she'd started to wonder if "orphaned at six" was listed in the science books alongside leprosy. Her situation felt like a disease, spreading and growing worse each time she moved from one foster family to another. She'd become a shadow to everyone but the local police, who'd started appearing in her teenage life with regular frequency.

But she wasn't a teenager anymore. Dr. Katherine Arnold had walked away from the labels that had tormented her throughout high school—orphan and troublemaker. At eighteen, she'd packed everything she owned in an industrial strength trash bag and headed for the one place that wanted her. College. A perfect SAT score and a heartfelt essay offered a way out of the town than had branded her unworthy.

Now, she'd returned looking so different that no one would connect Dr. Katherine Arnold with Kat, the juvenile delinquent orphan from the wrong side of town. Not that she'd ever planned to return to Oregon. But when Dr. Westbury, her mentor and the doctor in charge of her clinical trial, broke her ankle, Kat had packed her bags and agreed to fill in for the esteemed neurologist.

Kat could have called off the trip and pulled Josh Summers from the trail. The severity of his accident and subsequent symptoms didn't exactly line up with the rest of the patients in the trial. Kat had a feeling Dr. Westbury had noted Josh Summer's address and envisioned a relaxing trip through Oregon wine country. Instead, Kat had boarded the plane, determined to show Independence Falls that she'd succeeded despite the fact they'd cast her aside over and over.

But tonight, before they drove to his hometown, she wanted Brody to get to know the person she'd become. She wanted him to look at her for a few hours and see *her*. Not Dr. Katherine Arnold, his brother's doctor, or Kat, the awkward, friendless girl no one wanted to talk to growing up. Brody Summers would never mess around with his brother's doctor. And connecting the woman he'd wanted on the sidewalk with the girl who'd clung to the shadows as a teenager wouldn't help.

For the first time in her life, Kat felt as if fate was handing her a fairy tale—a few carefree hours with the man of her dreams. Summoning the you-can't-intimidate-me attitude she'd fine-tuned in college and perfected in medical school, she stepped into the bar. And Brody reached for his phone.

Moving toward the empty bar stool at his side, Kat's gaze fixed on her old crush. He was reading a text message.

"Shit," he muttered, setting the phone down and lifting his pint glass to his lips.

Kat rested her hands on the back of the leather bar stool beside him. "You don't look like a man ready to celebrate his amazing recovery."

Brody glanced over his shoulder. His mouth formed a line thin. The look in his deep brown eyes . . .

Kat caught herself before instinct pushed her to run. The agony staring back at her was too familiar.

His brow furrowed. "My recovery?"

"From your tumble on the sidewalk?" She forced a smile, though she knew from experience that laughter and teasing didn't help, not when pain had a choke hold on your emotions. Still, halfhearted jokes were sometimes the only defense. "Did the hotel shower erase the aches?"

"I'm fine."

You're lying.

She pulled the stool away from the bar. "Mind if I join you?"

He stared at her hands, resting on the back of the bar stool. For a second she wondered if he'd reach out, covering her hand with his.

"I'm not good company tonight," he said finally. "Just came down for a beer."

"But the fact that you're here, in the bar, tells me you didn't want to be alone."

"I called room service, but the wait was over an hour."

Kat slid onto the leather seat. Out of the corner of her eye she saw Brody's too serious gaze drop to her skirt, watching the fabric slide up her thighs. She signaled the bored young woman behind the bar who'd spent every minute since Kat had walked in with her fingers dancing over the keys on her tablet. "A glass of Oregon pinot noir, please."

Brody's phone vibrated and he scooped it off the bar, scanning another message on the screen.

"Good news?"

"No." He set the cell down and looked over at her. His

lips parted but he hesitated as if debating how much to tell this woman he still believed to be a total stranger. "I'm part of the volunteer search and rescue squad. A family visiting from out of state—mom, dad, and two kids ages twelve and ten—went for a hike on Mount Hood a few days ago and never came back. We found the parents and the twelve-year-old this morning. Dehydrated and hungry, but otherwise OK. No sign of the younger kid. According to his parents, their son fell off a ledge. They left the trail to find him, but got lost."

Kat nodded, her mind calculating the time frame, potential injuries, and the child's age. Based on those details, the outlook wasn't good.

"Have you worked search and rescue for long?" she asked.

"Five years all in. But lately I've been going out on more searches. I just started helping teams in other counties. I guess I'm new to the big rescues. In the past, I did a lot of sprained ankles and lost hikers. When I had the time to go out at all."

"It takes a while." She raised her wineglass and took a sip. "To separate your work, the job you need to do, from the fact that a child might die."

Brody studied her as if trying to blend his vision of a first responder with her skirt and heels.

"I worked in the ER at a New York City hospital." *A rotation in medical school.* But he didn't need the details of her résumé, not right now.

"You're a doctor?"

She nodded, leaving out *and I also have a Ph.D.* He'd find out in the morning when he went to pick up Dr. Westbury, the neurologist who he believed would be treating his brother—and came face-to-face with her. Right now, it sounded like Brody Summers needed someone to listen. Nothing more.

Shoving her teenage fantasies aside, Kat focused on the man buried in worry for a lost child.

Oh hell, he's still perfect, ready to rush in and save the day. Only he's moved beyond Super Gluing sneakers.

Lust fought for control, but she pushed the pesky, physical feelings aside. Right now she needed to do something to help Brody Summers climb out of the pit of worry and dread he'd dug for himself.

"I know the feeling of doing everything you possibly can for a kid and still losing," she said. "The first time, I was convinced I'd failed. The little girl was only five years and we tried everything. She was in a coma for four days. It felt like forever. But the whole time, I kept thinking this must be so much worse for the family. I was the one who could do something about it. I had the training. If only I could be there, at her side more, or come up with a way to save her—"

And wow, that was so much more than she'd planned to share. It had been a long time since she thought about that kid.

"What happened?" Brody asked, his brow knit with concern.

"We lost her. The worst part was facing the parents

to deliver the bad news. In that moment, you realize it doesn't matter that you tried every trick in the book. At the end of the day you still failed and their baby is gone." She took a sip of her wine, carefully setting the glass back on the bar. "And that was the wrong story to tell right now. I sent plenty of patients home to their families, healed and happy."

"I haven't done everything." Brody glanced at the lobby, ignoring her disclaimer. "I should be out there searching, making sure the kid gets reunited with his parents."

"Your shift ended?" she guessed.

"Yeah. The team leader in this area plays by the rules. He wants everyone searching the mountain rested. I told him to call me if they need more hands later, once I'd had a break. And the guys still out there are sending updates. So I'll find out when it's over."

He turned his focus back to his drink, his jaw still tight with frustration. "Can I ask you something?"

"Sure." She took a long drink from her wine. When she'd daydreamed about seeing Brody Summers again, she'd skipped over the depressing-conversation-in-a-generic-hotel-bar fantasy. She'd imagined a wanting smile as he pulled his shirt over his head. But fate was up to her old tricks again, offering her the man of her dreams buried in concern for a child. Sex was probably the last thing on this man's mind.

"Ask away," she said.

"How did you cope when your everything wasn't

enough?" His brown eyes stared into hers. "When you lost a child?"

I counted down the days until the end of my ER rotation and I hit the gym.

But she had a feeling Brody Summers, Mr. I'll Help Save Your Sneakers, wasn't ready to give up search and rescue.

"Did you bring a swimsuit?" she asked, her imagination running full speed ahead. Brody Summers in a swimsuit, every inch of his muscular upper body on display . . .

She mentally slammed the door, knowing she needed to draw the line at looking tonight. But she could still offer a way to work off the building fears for a child and his frustration at being sidelined.

"I'm only here one night," Brody said. "Why?"

"Boxers or briefs?" she asked.

"What?" His eyebrows shot up, his brown eyes widening.

"I'm going somewhere with this." Maybe not back to the king-size bed in her hotel room, but tonight she would have to settle for Brody Summers dripping wet in his underwear.

And the knowledge that she'd stepped in and helped him this time.

"Boxers."

"I know just what you need." Kat signaled the bartender for the check. "A little late night exercise to take your mind off the things you can't change."

"Exercise?" His brown eyes glanced down at her legs.

OK, so maybe sex wasn't the very last thing on his mind.

"In the hotel pool," she said.

Kat slid off the bar stool and headed for the lobby. Pausing on the carpet, she glanced back at Brody. He'd pulled out his wallet and tossed a few bills on the bar. Slowly, he slipped it into his back pocket and looked up at her. The pain she'd witnessed in his brown eyes lingered.

Kat stepped onto the hardwood floor, knowing he'd follow her. Whatever happened in the morning when he learned she'd replaced Dr. Westbury, tonight would be worth the repercussions if she could ease his concern for that lost child.

Seeing Brody Summers in his underwear, that was just a bonus. And where she had to draw the line. There would be no peeking beneath. Not tonight. Unless he was wearing white boxers . . .

She turned to face him. Raising an eyebrow, he stopped by her side. His large mountain-man muscles made the hallway leading to the pool feel small and cramped. Away from the bar, he seemed steady and sure.

Maybe she'd imagined his need for a late night dip in the pool? But then his questioning gaze locked with hers and she saw the barely leashed frustration that he wasn't out on that mountain.

"What color are you boxers?" she demanded.

His brow furrowed as if he was beginning to question her sanity. "I'm not sure—"

A buzzing noise followed by a ring interrupted. Brody glanced down at the phone in his hand.

"A text?" she said.

Brody gave a curt nod as he lifted the phone, his fingers moving over the screen. "From one of the guys on the rescue squad."

"Whatever it says," she said softly, "it's not your fault. You did your job and sometimes that is all you can do. I need you to trust me on this. Bad news rips into you, but you can't let it tear you apart. OK?"

He nodded as he read the message, and she wondered if he'd heard her. She could feel the tension radiating off him.

"They found him." Brody leaned his head back and closed his eyes. "The ten-year-old kid. He has a broken ankle from the fall. He's scared and dehydrated. But he's alive. He's on his way to the hospital now."

"That's good." Kat ran her hands over her skirt. His relief was palpable. And she shared the feeling. She'd witnessed parents free-falling into grief when a child's well-being hung on the line. Knowing crisis had been averted—for the family, for the little boy, and for the rescuers—she felt as if a physical weight had been lifted from her shoulders, even though she'd never met this family.

"I guess you don't need that swim after all," she said.

"Kat." Brody opened his eyes, his gaze connecting with hers.

The pain she'd witnessed at the bar had faded into the background, replaced by a flare of desire so primal and fierce that her body tingled as if he'd run his hands over her.

"How did you celebrate?" he asked, his tone low and rough. Oh goodness, she wanted to hear him whisper dirty things in her ear all night. And she wanted to see him stripped down to his boxers.

"When your best was enough and everything turned out OK," he continued, his gaze running over her. "What did you do?"

"Sometimes . . ." she murmured, the heat and wanting trampling her common sense like a herd of elephants.

Brody had allowed relief to open the door to lust. She knew she couldn't take her walking, talking fantasy to bed like this. But she couldn't resist a chance to flirt with her crush for a little while, free from the pain that had pulled at him since he'd left the mountain.

" . . . sometimes," she continued, "I like to celebrate with a swim."

Chapter 3

BRODY PARKED HIS willpower in the hall and led the blond doctor through the door marked Pool. If his brothers saw him now they would laugh their asses off. He'd driven up to Portland to save two families—the stranded hikers and his own. Instead, he was taking an emergency room doctor who probably sent the men of New York City racing to the ER with a long list of fake ailments for a swim. But he couldn't walk away.

Beyond her beautiful face, he'd witnessed the relief in her eyes when she'd learned that the kid was safe. One look at her and something inside him had snapped. For the past few months he'd navigated a boatload of stress through choppy waters. And heck, he wanted a break.

His grip on her hand tightened, his mind focused on the here and now. The feel of her soft skin. The sound of her breathing, which quickened as they moved through door. Every sound she made suggested her desire matched his, poised to spiral out of control.

A few paces into the warm and thankfully empty pool room, he turned to face her. Her breath caught as he stared into her eyes. Hesitation? Heck, maybe she'd read his mind and knew he wanted to bypass the pool, taking her straight to his bed.

"Brody, if you're having second thoughts, we can head back into the hall and call it a night. But if you want to stay and, um, celebrate, I promise I won't take advantage of you in your underwear." She spoke in a low tone that left part of his body hoping he could convince Little Miss Perfect to break her word.

"And if I can't make the same promise?" he challenged. The past twenty-four hours—heck, the past few months—had chipped away at his calm logic and left him emotionally rung out. He felt as if he was standing on the edge of wild.

"That won't be a problem."

The way she said those words—she might as well have wrapped her hand around his dick.

But instead of reaching for the part of his body threatening to wage a war against what remained of his common sense, she released his hand. "Wait here."

Brody watched her move toward a metal closet, taking in the pool room's layout. A line of lounge chairs filled the space to their left. Along the wall to the right stood a table stacked with towels. Next to the pile, a shower and a sign that clearly stated all guests swam at their own risk. Brody glanced at the long narrow pool that ran the length of the room. The stairs leading to the shallow end stood directly in front of him. And in the corner opposite the entrance sat a hot tub, steam rising from the swirling water.

He bit back a low growl as images filled his mind. Kat stripping off her clothes and joining him in the steaming water . . .

"Where are you going?" he asked, returning his attention to the present as she opened the door. She rummaged for a moment and turned around, triumphant.

"To find this." She held up a sign that read POOL CLOSED.

Her heels clicked against the cement pool deck as she headed to the door. Poking her head out, she scanned the hall and then slipped the sign into place.

"Just in case someone else wants to celebrate," she said.

"You know all the tricks," he murmured. "Have you done this before?"

"When I was a teenager, I occasionally snuck into places I wasn't supposed to be. I got caught once and learned my lesson. Most people obey a Closed sign."

She settled onto a lounge chair. Planting her palms on the cushion, she leaned back and crossed the long legs he'd admired earlier while lying at her feet. Her skirt slid up her thighs, stopping short of offering a peekaboo glance underneath.

"You're just going to sit there and watch?"

"I can close my eyes while you undress if you're feeling shy. But I can't promise I won't peek."

He tried to remember the last time a woman had toyed with him and came up blank. Back home, he might as well have had the word "serious" tattooed on his forehead. Women looked at him and saw long-term. And yeah, he liked being that guy, the one people knew they could count on. When it came to his family, he wouldn't have it any other way. But sometimes—like when he wanted a chance to explore a beautiful blonde's long legs without worrying about the long-term picture—it was just plain lonely.

"I'm not shy," he said.

"Then lose the clothes, Brody."

He pulled his Moore Timber T-shirt over his head and tossed it aside. Stealing a glance at his audience, he saw her green eyes widen. She uncrossed her legs, drawing his attention to the smooth skin of her thighs. His gaze traveled up her body, leaving him wondering what lie beneath her silky shirt.

"I hope you're not shy," he said, his voice low and wanting, a solid reflection on how he felt. "Because I want to watch."

"Tempting. But this is your celebration. I think I should stay on the sidelines and play lifeguard." Her sultry tone left him wondering what she sounded like in bed.

"You're worried I'll need saving?" He released his belt buckle and undid his pants before realizing he needed to remove his boots first. Maybe he would need her to come to his rescue.

"What if you push yourself to the point of exhaustion?"

"I know my limits." And he'd never come anywhere close to them, not on a rescue, or in the bedroom. Seeing the way she stared at him—as if the universe would grant her the X-ray vision to peek beneath his black boxers if she looked long and hard—he wondered: would her limits line up with his? Just how far was she willing to take this game?

"Sure you don't want to join me?" He looked her straight in the eye, letting her see how damn much he wanted to get her wet.

"My underwear isn't exactly appropriate for swimming."

Show me. Let me decide.

Knowing he was seconds away from demanding that she strip, Brody turned and headed for the pool. He needed to slip into the lukewarm water before he proposed a different kind of celebration.

"Brody, wait."

He paused, one hand gripping the railing. "Change your mind about playing lifeguard?" he growled.

"That sign clearly states you need a shower before entering the water." She nodded to the list posted below the Swim at Your Own Risk warning.

"Do you always follow the rules?" he challenged.

"I've broken my fair share. When I was younger. These days, I try to do as I'm told."

Brody blinked. He barely knew Kat. Still, obedient was the last word that came to mind when he thought about the woman who'd knocked him over with a suitcase and demanded that he strip by the pool.

But the lust rising up didn't give a damn. The mental image was already lodged in his head. Kat on his bed, her wrists bound, waiting for him to spell out what he wanted . . .

Turning on his heels, he headed for the shower. With one turn of the knob, ice cold water poured out of the showerhead. He moved underneath, biting back a curse as the shower's spray ran over his mostly naked body. But the need to challenge her words refused to wash away.

He'd always held back, giving the women he'd dated what they wanted. But he'd never taken. He'd never issued commands. In bed and out, he put the people he cared about first. He shouldered other people's problems—listening, caring, and fixing.

Brody stepped forward, the cold stream rushing down his back. Running his hands over his face, he wiped away the water and opened his eyes. He looked over at Kat. Every muscle in her body appeared tense, as if she were waiting for an invitation to leap up from the chair and join him in the shower.

Her desire matched his. He could see it plain as day in her eyes. Control slipped away, followed by the tight hold his sense of duty had on his life. His world narrowed to one thought—claim Little Miss Perfect. Tonight, for one night, make her his.

THE SOUND OF running water hitting the cement floor echoed against the tiled walls. Beneath the noise, Kat swore she heard Brody let out a low growl. The man was standing in a cold shower, and judging from the way his wet underwear clung to his body, she'd dialed the lust up to an eleven.

I try to do as I'm told.

She'd been teasing him when she'd said those words. These days, she rarely took orders from anyone. The high-profile neurologist leading her clinical trial? Maybe. A man she wanted to see without his boxer briefs? Never. She'd fought too long and hard for control over her life to let anyone call the shots.

But seeing Brody's reaction, she wondered if she could pretend until sunrise. *If* he invited her back to his room. And *if* she went.

Kat shifted on the lounge chair. As if he'd sensed her movement, Brody opened his eyes and looked right at her. And just like that her mind bypassed the shower and headed straight for the bedroom. He'd told her that he knew his own limits. But what if she pushed past his breaking point? Would he give in to the raw lust radiating from his hard body?

Brody turned off the shower and reached for a towel, quickly securing it around his waist. Still dripping wet, he walked over to the chair. Her breath caught as he closed the space between them.

"I don't want a celebration swim," he said.

"You don't?" Heat pulsed from his wet body, but his words raised alarm bells. She'd misread his desire. He was done playing games and wanted to go back to his room. Or have another beer, toasting to a successful mission.

"I want you, Kat."

Those words, on his lips—they blew her fantasies away. Molten desire rushed over her, every nerve in her body doing a little happy dance while chanting, *Brody Summers wants you!*

His hands cupped her jaw as she stood to meet him. He studied her lips as if the only question was *how* to kiss her, not *if* he should. His lips hovering over hers, she closed her eyes, waiting for his kiss.

"Is there anything I should know?"

His low, rough voice sent another rush of need over her. She opened her eyes and saw his kiss-me-now fever staring back at her.

"A boyfriend in New York?" he added.

"No boyfriend." Logically, she knew now was the time to tell him why she'd traveled across the country. But she wanted to spend a few hours knowing Brody Summers desired *her*. She was close to cementing her place among the top neurologists in the country, but that didn't change the fact that once upon a time she'd gone to bed in a house that never felt like home, wishing like crazy that this man would notice her.

"Kiss me, Brody."

Running his fingers through her hair, he claimed her lips. As if her command had granted him permission to race past soft and gentle, his tongue swept into her mouth exploring, tasting, demanding . . .

She leaned against his solid body. One of his hands abandoned her hair, to wrap around her waist. He held her tight against him, allowing her to fall deeper and deeper into his kiss. She'd never melted into a man's embrace, letting him take and take and take. But with Brody, she turned to butter. Pressed against him, she felt so turned on, so feminine, and so . . . wet.

He broke away. But his hands held her close, the dampness from his shower seeping into her clothes as his gaze met hers. For a fleeting second those deep brown depths offered a window into his thoughts. A fierce wanting stared back at her. A look like that led down a dead-end street. The only thing waiting at the end?

Toe-curling orgasms.

"I'll tell you mine," she said, running her hands over his shoulders to his biceps, giving them a light, playful squeeze. His muscles demanded exploration. And she wanted to touch and taste every inch of him. "If you tell me yours."

He raised an eyebrow. "My what?"

"Your mental picture for how tonight plays out."

One hand moved over her jaw, down her throat, teasing every nerve along the way until he reached the first button of her shirt. "You first."

She rose up on her tiptoes and brushed her lips against his ear. Releasing his arm, she reached for the impressive bulge beneath the flimsy hotel towel. "I want to push past your limits, drive you wild. Right here, in the pool, or in your bed. You choose the setting, just don't hold back."

"My room." Brody drew her hand away from his erection. He stepped back and began pulling his clothes on as if someone had pulled the fire alarm. "And once I have you there, I'm going to run my mouth over every inch of you. Hell, right now I just plain want you, Kat."

Tomorrow, when he learned the truth, she might regret her lies by omission. But right now, with those words echoing in her head, she set aside the obstacles. Brody Summers wanted her. For tonight, that was everything.

"Brody, tonight I want to be your fantasy."

Chapter 4

STANDING UNDER THE hotel hallway's fluorescent lights, Kat's words roared in his ears.

I want to be your fantasy.

He'd had the occasional one-night stand, though not recently and always with women outside of Independence Falls. But he'd never been drawn to a woman like this, feeling as if he needed to claim every inch of her and make her come until sunrise. And he sure as hell had never shared his fantasies before. But tonight he'd kissed control good-bye. He'd let her in, and damn if she hadn't said the words he'd been dying to hear.

The elevator doors opened and Brody stepped inside, holding tight to Kat's hand.

He could feel her gaze on him, but he kept his eyes fixed on the control panel as he pressed 3. One look at her and temptation would win. He'd hit the Stop button, drawing the elevator to a halt between floors, and taste every inch of her right here.

"You're eyeing that big red button as if you're thinking of doing something naughty," she said, her tone light and playful.

Her words were the final straw, breaking the dam, allowing his self-control to rush away. When he'd read the text at the bar, relief had breached his restraint. Knowing that kid was out there alone while he sat in the hotel, removed from the action, he'd felt so freaking helpless. And yeah, that was unfamiliar ground for him. He hadn't realized how much he needed the ten-year-old to be found alive, safe and sound, until his phone delivered the news.

Now he just plain *needed*.

"Tell me," she said. "Tell me what you're thinking."

Ignoring the elevator buttons, Brody pressed her back against the wall. He placed one hand beside her head, careful to leave space between their bodies. One touch and he might sink to his knees, taking her skirt with him.

"I left my control by the pool," he said, his voice low and rough. "So if you're expecting restraint, if you wanted me to make love to you, I'm not the guy for you. Maybe tomorrow, but not tonight. When the elevator opens, you can walk away, and I'll understand."

He pressed a kiss to her neck, needing to taste her again, now, before they reached the third floor. If she ran, he wouldn't blame her. But God help him, he wanted her to stay.

"I'm going to make you come. You have my word on

that. I'm dying to touch you, taste you, learn what turns you on and makes you scream for more so damn loud the entire hotel knows you're mine tonight. But—"

The bell sounded and the elevator opened, indicating they'd reached his floor. He stepped back, extending his arm to hold the door open, allowing her the space to decide.

"What's your room number, Brody?" Kat stepped out, glancing over her shoulder. "After that little speech, you owe me an orgasm."

BRODY SUMMERS PAID his debts. She should remember that for the next time she wanted something from his man. But with her back against the door to his hotel room, his mouth covering hers and his fingers pulling at the buttons on her shirt, the here and now took precedence over the future.

Her hands moved over his shoulders, up his neck, working their way into his short brown hair. She wanted to believe she was holding his lips against hers. But she had a feeling it was the other way around.

Alone in his hotel room, removed from the question of were they doing this, he kissed her as if making out was a contact sport. His lower body rocked against her, mimicking the motions of his tongue thrusting into her mouth. His fingers released the last button and his hands ran over her abdomen, pausing to tease her breasts through the lacy fabric of her bra. Kat arched her back, seeking more from his touch. And Brody delivered, drawing the lacy cups down, allowing his palms to brush back and forth over her nipples.

She ran her hands over his arms, determined to keep his touch leading her eager body to the edge of a full-body orgasm. She knew what she wanted and she wasn't afraid to offer a little touch-me-here guidance.

But he was too fast. Abandoning her breasts—*no, no, no!*—he caught hold of her wrists, drawing them down to her sides.

"Brody," she protested, pulling away from his kiss.

"I gave you my word."

Taking her lower lip between his teeth, he stripped her black shirt off. The feeling of the silky fabric moving over her skin sent shivers up and down her arms. Tossing the shirt onto his shoulder, he focused on the front clasp of her bra.

He struggled with the plastic closure. Anticipation swelled as his fingers brushed back and forth over her bare skin and she debated helping him.

The clasp gave and he slipped her bra off, tossing it behind him. His palms covered her breasts and she closed her eyes, leaning into him.

"So damn perfect." He released his hold, sliding his hands around to the back of her skirt. He conquered her zipper on the first try, and her skirt fell to the floor at her feet.

Brody didn't waste a second, sliding the black thong down her legs. "Step out," he ordered.

WILD WITH YOU   33

She obeyed, and her panties followed her bra into the dark area beyond his hotel room's entryway.

"Put your hands behind your back," he said.

"Planning to tie me up?" She'd never ventured into bondage games. Offering control during sex, or anywhere else, had never appealed to her.

"Yes." He pressed a kiss to her neck.

"Do we need a safe word?" she gasped, savoring the feel of his mouth on her skin.

"No." His gaze met hers, his brown eyes deep dark pools of need. She could get lost just looking at him, her world narrowing down to Brody and desire. Nothing more. Maybe she already was.

"If you say no at any point," he continued, "if you tell me to stop, I will. You can trust me on that."

"OK."

Oh yes, she'd fallen head over heels into desire.

He guided her hands into position and her body responded to the contact. One touch and her breasts begged to be next. Need pulsed through her, leaving her aching to press her thighs together. The firm line separating her likes from dislikes blurred.

Brody turned her on, plain and simple. Tonight, he was pushing his limits. And she wanted to do the same.

Holding her wrists behind her lower back with one hand, he pulled her shirt off his shoulder and proceeded to wrap it around her wrists, weaving an intricate knot. Giving the fabric a quick tug, he tested his handiwork. It held, pinning her arms behind her.

"But I want to touch you too," she said. She'd spent years dreaming about his muscles. Having them on display, within reach, but unable to touch? It wasn't fair.

"My turn first," he murmured. His hands moved away from the knot and he stepped back, his eyes meeting hers. "Tell me if this is too much for you and I'll let you go."

But she didn't want him to send her away. Not tonight. Save the distance for the morning. "I want to be here," she said. "With you. I want this."

His brown eyes stared into hers. He'd stripped away her clothes, but he didn't look down. It was as if seeing her reactions, reading the emotion in her eyes, mattered more to him than the sight of her bared breasts.

"Spread your legs for me, Kat." His fingers brushed the inside of her right thigh, blazing a trail, higher and higher, and she obeyed. Moving her feet apart, she offered him access.

"First, I want to feel you come against my hand." He abandoned her thigh, pressing his thumb against the part of her body most likely to transform his words into reality. "With your hands tied, your back up against the door, I want to learn what you like."

His eyes never left hers as he drew small, teasing circles over her clit. The intensity of his gaze combined with the deep, rough timbre of his voice, sent her body swirling toward a place of unfamiliar intimacy.

"And then?" she whispered.

"After I learn whether you like a soft teasing touch or pressure moving back and forth over you," he said, his fingers following his words, swiping back and forth over the one part of her body that could make her come right now with only his thumb. "After I find out if you need to feel me inside of you, to turn you on, to get you there," he continued, drawing his hand down past her clit as he slipped a finger inside her. "I want to kneel down at your feet."

She gasped as her body tightened around him, taking what he offered but wanting more. Her eyelids fluttered shut, focusing on the thrust of his finger, in and out. His thumb alternated between pressing against her and teasing her with feather-light touches.

"Open your eyes, Kat. I want to know you're with me."

"I am. Oh God, I am with you." She met his gaze as he added a second finger. "What comes next?"

"I lick you until you come against my mouth."

"Hmm," she murmured, searching for the power to form words as his wicked touch brought her oh so close to an orgasm. "I like your plan. But it won't work. I need your cock."

"Is that a challenge?" he growled.

"It's the truth." She'd wanted him for so long. And now that they were here, touching exploring, naked—her not him, but she held on to her hope they'd get there too—she needed all of him.

"We'll see about that."

Desire rose up, threatening to take over her body as his fingers thrust into her. He continued his merciless strokes, back and forth, adapting his touch with every groan. His eyes remained focused on hers as if daring her to try and hide the fact that he'd delivered her to this point. Right now, Brody Summers owned her pleasure.

"You may want my cock, but you don't need it," he murmured. "Look at you, ready to come so hard. Kat, you're stunning."

His words coupled with the sincerity written in his intense gaze to push her over the edge. A take-no-prisoners orgasm swept over her, claiming all her senses.

"Don't look away," he said as her head leaned back.

She kept her eyes open, letting him see everything. The power of his touch, the awe at how his man took her by surprise—he made her feel so damn *wanted*. It was a fleeting feeling. She knew that. But with her arms bound, his fingers demanding all the pleasure she had to give, she clung to the foreign sensation.

"You win," she gasped as the orgasm receded. Her hands pulled at her knotted shirt. "You can untie me now."

Withdrawing his hand, Brody shook his head. "I'm not done with you yet. You can say no, but first—"

He dropped to his knees, one hand guiding her right leg over his shoulder. Balanced on one high-heel-clad foot, she wobbled. Her hands struggled to keep her from toppling over. His fingers wrapped around her hips, his broad shoulders pinning her against the door.

"Lean on me," he said. "I've got you."

His tongue replaced his hands, teasing the parts of her body still reeling from her orgasm, and all her rational thought slipped away.

TONIGHT WAS FILLED with firsts. First time he'd stripped to his underwear beside the hotel pool. First time he'd run his tongue over a woman whose last name he didn't know. He'd had flings before, but never like this. Tonight the intensity was off the charts. And it was the first time he'd unleashed every last desire, tying a woman's wrists allowing him to focus on her pleasure.

Judging from the look in her eyes when she'd come, Kat needed this too. Nothing holding him back from showing her how much he wanted to hear her scream his name again and again—

"Brody!"

He flicked his tongue over her, alternating the pressure. Savoring the taste of her, the feel of her smooth skin against his mouth, he held her tight. She was his. Beautiful, sexy Little Miss Perfect's every cry, every moan, belonged to him right now.

Her hips bucked against his mouth, seeking more. He followed her lead, letting her rock against his tongue, allowing her to roll her hips. The leg resting on his shoulder tensed.

"Oh God!" She dug her heel into his back, her body shaking as she fell apart against his mouth.

His hand moved around to her back, squeezing her ass once. Releasing his hold as her cries echoed in the cramped entryway to his hotel, he reached for her hand. His fingers interlaced with hers.

Her climax peaked. The movement of her hips against his mouth slowed, and her cries died down as she gasped for air. Through it all he held her hand.

"Brody?" She slid her leg off his shoulder and turned, pulling her fingers free from his. With her perfect ass near his mouth, he was tempted to steal a taste.

"Untie me," she demanded.

He stood and reached for the designer clothing holding her wrists together.

"Now," she added, looking over her shoulder at him. "It's my turn."

He groaned, his cock pressing against his fly, begging to be released as her shirt fell to the floor. Whirling around, she reached for his crotch, pressing her palm against him.

"I think you're going to like payback." She gave his eager cock a pat and stepped back. "Take off your—"

The piercing ring of his cell phone interrupted. The vibration against his thigh, so close to his dick, shocked the hell out him. He scrambled to retrieve it. His brother's name flashed on the screen.

"I need to take this." He swiped his finger across the screen, moving away from her. "Chad? This better be important."

"Josh is gone," his easygoing middle brother snapped.

"What do you mean gone?" Brody demanded.

"I stopped by the house to check on him before Georgia and Eric's rehearsal dinner. I wanted to see if he was getting along with that nursing student you hired to watch over him. And to ask if he'd changed his mind about going to the party tonight now that we'd sprung him from the rehab center. He's only been home for a week. I thought he'd be itching to get out and see people," Chad said. "I didn't think he'd run and hide."

Brody heard footsteps on the other end, the sound of doors opening and closing. The farmhouse he and his siblings called home had been in the family for generations. They'd grown up playing hide and seek, racing up and down the stairs. Josh's short-term memory had disappeared in the wake of the accident, but his youngest brother still knew every inch of the house. "You've checked all the hiding spots?"

"I know this house as well as he does, Brody." A door slammed in the background. "And I can't fucking find him. Unless he took a hike, he's around here somewhere. His truck is still parked out front. Hell, so is the new girl's sedan."

"Check the barn and the studio apartment," Brody said. He had a pretty good idea where Josh had gone. "And call me back. I'll be waiting by my phone."

Not getting a blowjob from the woman he could still taste on his lips.

Brody turned to face Kat. "I'm sorry."

"That wasn't about the kid on the mountain."

Her fingers made quick work of the buttons on her shirt. And she'd also slipped back into her skirt.

"No," he said. "My younger brother was in an accident. He's had a rough recovery. He insisted we move him back home. But . . ."

His voice trailed off. She didn't need to know the details of Josh's short-term memory loss, or the depression that had followed.

"And now he's missing," she said.

"Yeah, but he didn't go far. The cars are still there. So is his caregiver, I'm guessing."

"And chances are they're together."

"Yes." Together and doing the things he wished he could do to her. But just in case Josh had wandered off into the woods surrounding his family's property, or taken one of his sister's rescue horses for a joy ride, Brody needed to wait by the phone. Heck, he'd drive down and start looking himself if he didn't needed to be here to pick up the famous Dr. Westbury in the morning.

"I should go," she said.

"Wait." Brody stepped forward. The thought of watching the door close behind her without the promise of more felt downright wrong. Chalk it up to the fact that part of him still wanted her—her mouth on him, her legs wrapped around his waist as he slipped inside her. Or credit the fact that his desires lined up pretty damn well with hers, and one night wasn't enough. Not even close.

"How long are you in town?" he asked, glancing around the room. He found a pad of paper with the hotel logo across the top and a matching pen on the desk. He quickly wrote his name and number on the top sheet, tore it off and held it out to her. "I'd like to see you again."

Surprise stared back at him. Shit, maybe she'd only wanted a few hours with him. That thought stung, probably more than it should.

But then a smile, edged with sadness, replaced her wide-eyed shock, and she took the paper from his hand.

"You'll be seeing me again soon, Brody."

Chapter 5

KAT SLID THE key card into the door while mentally
listing the things she'd lost in Brody Summer's hotel
room. Her control—she'd tossed that aside the minute
he stripped her down and tied her up. Her plan to offer
comfort, to listen to his problems—as soon as he learned
the kid was safe, she'd abandoned her good intentions.

And last, but not least, her underwear.

Opening the door, Kat headed for the king-sized bed,
flopped down on her stomach and buried her face in
the pillows. She'd left her black lace thong behind. But
the minutes after he'd received a call about his missing
brother, also known as her future patient, hardly felt like
the time to ask for help finding her panties. And she was
admittedly still rattled from the way he'd taken over,
calling the shots and issuing commands.

Spread your legs for me, Kat.

She'd never in a million years expected one night

with the man who'd patiently helped glue her only pair of shoes together would turn into *that*. After learning about the lost kid, she had planned to sideline her Brody Summers fantasies, not jump on board with his. What happened in his room wasn't an *oops, we gave into a mutual desire* thing. He'd opened up to her, letting her in. To his sexual fantasies, sure, but it was a step beyond casual sex.

She'd mastered the one-night stand in college, perfecting the art of pushing men away before they left her. But they'd never been like this. The connection. The need. The trust. The orgasms. The night she'd experienced left her standing on shaky ground with a man she had to face in the morning.

Tomorrow she had to reveal the reason for her trip, and endure an awkward two-hour drive in this state that spelled out bad memories. One hundred twenty minutes spent wondering what would have happened if Brody's brother hadn't interrupted earlier. Two hours of trying to guess if the man who'd tied her up and delivered back-to-back orgasms regretted their time together, or wanted more.

The thought of Brody's tall, muscular frame seated behind the wheel, steering his vehicle down the road while silently wishing he'd stayed at the bar last night far, far away from her—that mental picture cut into her like a knife opening an old wound.

"What is it about this state?" she murmured, tossing the pillow aside. She set foot in Oregon and the old hurts she'd buried here long ago resurfaced, driving her to make choices that in hindsight looked downright stupid.

She wasn't an orphan clinging to a desperate hope that someone would like her enough to offer a place to call home. Back in Manhattan, she lived in a high rise. Her two-bedroom apartment probably cost more than the largest house in Independence Falls. Work drove her life. She'd earned her colleagues' respect as she'd climbed closer and closer to the top of her field. A specialty she'd selected because it was one of the most challenging. She didn't need the people out here to like her.

And she couldn't afford to melt into a puddle of desire just because Brody Summers said the words she'd longed to hear—*I want you.*

But she had. Oh God, she had. And now she had to live with the repercussions. Only it would be so much harder than she'd imagined.

I'd like to see you again.

But she couldn't get involved with him. Never mind that she was treating his brother, her life was waiting for her back in New York. She had her job and the little girl she mentored.

OK, maybe Brianna wasn't the best example of her ties to the East Coast. The ten-year-old girl barely spoke to her during their bimonthly lunches. But that hadn't stopped Kat from daydreaming about becoming a larger part of the foster child's life. Trips to museums. Central park in nice weather. They could go shopping for clothes and toys.

But even if her relationship with Brianna never moved beyond sullen lunches, Kat knew she couldn't start something with Brody. As much as she wanted to even the orgasm count, she knew better than most people that wishes crashed and burned every day, especially in Oregon. One more I-can't-resist-him moment and this one would detonate, threatening her carefully constructed life.

"WHAT WERE YOU thinking?" Brody demanded, the phone pressed to his ear.

Swinging his duffel over his other shoulder, he gave the hotel room a quick survey. Black lace peeked out from behind the desk chair. Dropping to one knee, he picked Kat's underwear off the floor.

One more reason for her to call. . .

But he didn't want Kat to reach out looking for her panties. He wanted her to pick up the phone driven by desire to see him again.

"I haven't gotten laid in eight months," Josh said. "I thought now might be a good time to do something about that."

Fucking irony. He stared at the slip of black lace in his hand. Last night he'd been thinking the same thing. Only it had been a lot longer than eight months. And they'd stopped short of the finish line because *someone* had gone missing.

"And you hired a twenty-something goddess to watch over me," Josh explained. "So I figured why not let her give me a full-body exam?"

"At least you remember what you did last night," Brody said. "That's something."

"I wrote it down. Nothing like waking up to a Post-it note about what the nursing student looks like naked."

"I hired her to make sure you didn't do anything stupid like turn on the gas stove and forget to switch it off," Brody said, pocketing the lace thong as he headed for the door. He needed to haul ass to the lobby in order to meet the doctor who would hopefully put an end to Josh's predicament. "Megan spent the last year taking care of Walter Kenny while working for her nursing degree. She had excellent references."

"Walter is an ornery old man. No wonder she wanted a roll in the hay."

Brody pushed the Down button and waited for an elevator. "Is that why you took her to the barn?"

"I didn't know when you were coming back," Josh said. "I figured there would be less chance of interruption out there."

"I'm not in town right now," he explained. "I'm in Portland picking up the neurologist who has a clinical trial dealing with memory loss."

"A trial?" Josh said. "Like an experimental drug or weird brain surgery?"

"No. It's a task-oriented therapy." Whatever the hell that meant. At this point, Dr. Westbury's methods were their last hope.

The elevator arrived and he stepped inside, holding the door open. "I need to go. But I'll be home in a couple of hours and with the doctor. Write that down."

"Got it."

"Below that write 'Don't touch Megan' in big block letters," he added, releasing the door.

Josh chuckled. "Sure thing. And Brody?"

"Yeah?"

"Thank you for finding this doctor. I hate living like this. Some days it seems like I'm getting better. But I can't tell. And that's so fucking depressing—"

The line cut out. Brody lowered his phone, his little brother's words slicing past his frustration. So Josh had screwed his caregiver and interrupted his own wild night with Kat. Unlike his brother, Brody remembered every detail of last night, from the way she'd looked with her arms bound behind her back to the feel of her hips bucking against his mouth as she came.

The memory of her screams, the way she'd said his name as if she needed him to push her over the edge, traveled south. The door opened and he tried to think of something else, anything besides Kat's naked body pressed against his hotel room door, and the fact that he had her panties in his pocket.

He didn't want to face his brother's new doctor with a hard-on pressing against his jeans. Given her long list of credentials, Dr. Westbury was probably twice his age. But he doubted the woman was blind. Something about those three little letters following the MD after her name—-Ph.D.—told him that Dr. Westbury was observant.

Heading for the reception area where they'd agreed to meet, Brody counted back from one hundred. This trick had served him well in high school, and was working for him now.

Until he saw the woman who had driven him wild last night.

Kat stood by the desk, one perfectly manicured hand holding her cell phone. Compared to yesterday's outfit, her starched white button-up blouse, black slacks, and gold flats that bore a closer resemblance to ballet slippers than shoes, looked conservative and plain. Business clothes, he realized. But her flashy luggage sat by her feet, setting her apart from the other travelers pulling their plain bags.

When she glanced up from her cell screen, he offered a wave and headed over. He wasn't about to hand over her underwear in the lobby. Still, he could say good morning and offer another apology for cutting their night short.

"I guess you were right," he said. "About seeing each other again."

"Hello, Brody." She gave him a small, tentative smile. He hadn't known her long, but something was off.

"Look, I'm meeting someone right now, but I meant what I said last night. I'd like to see you again. How long are you in Portland? Maybe we could grab dinner while you're here?"

She drew a deep, measured breath as her green eyes locked with his. And he braced for the rejection. *I'm too busy,* or *I'm not ready to get involved right now.* He'd used that one a time or two to break up with a woman who wanted more than he could give. Though he always said those words before they lost their clothes.

"Brody," she said slowly. "I work with Dr. Karen Westbury. I'm the person you're waiting for."

Either Kat had left her seduce-me-if-you-dare voice in her hotel room or the woman he'd tied up with her own shirt was his brother's doctor.

Brody shook his head. It wasn't possible. He'd told her about his brother. She would have said something.

"I'm sorry, Brody," she continued. "I should have told you last night. At the last minute, we decided I should be the one to handle Josh's case."

Brody blinked, shock rushed in rendering him as close to helpless as he'd ever been. And damn if he didn't hate the feeling.

"You knew who I was?" he said, disbelief seeping into his words.

"I grew up in Independence Falls," she said. "That's part of the reason Dr. Westbury felt I should be the one to treat your brother. And she broke her ankle. She had to have surgery yesterday. Rather than delay Josh's treatment and our trial, I agreed to fly out."

Heck, he should be grateful she'd taken the case. But realizing that Kat had known who he was the entire time and let him believe she was an ER doctor? Shock gave way to anger, the feeling coiling in the pit of his stomach. His arms dropped to his side, his hands forming tight fists. He glanced at the wooden panels lining the front of the reception desk, wishing he could punch through them. Because right now he needed a helluva lot more than a swim to take the edge off.

Chapter 6

KAT WATCHED HER words sink in, myriad emotions fighting for control of Brody's expression. She had a feeling he could count on one hand the number of people who'd seen him so angry that steam threatened to come out of his ears.

Lucky me.

But then she'd brought this on herself, holding back the truth last night. And her reasons for doing so—she'd wanted to live in a fairy tale for a few hours and feel wanted—no longer felt justified.

She watched as Brody drew a deep breath and the anger seemingly receded. He needed her. That much was clear. Not in his bed, but helping his brother. Even if he wanted to tell her to take a one-way trip to hell, he wouldn't let emotions overtake his responsibility.

Logic suggested she should admire his oh-so-noble

choice. But part of her wanted him to let his feelings win. She wished the idea of losing the woman who'd gone to his room last night to the label His Brother's Doctor made him howl with unleashed fury.

But one night—one meeting—did not lead to I-need-you emotions. That truth had haunted her for her entire life. No reason it would change now because she'd let Brody Summers give her a pair of orgasms. Sure, they were the Rolls-Royces of climaxes, but that didn't mean they could lead to more.

"I see," Brody said, his tone measured and even. His dark eyes, which had openly conveyed his need and desire last night, appeared guarded. "We should hit the road. My truck is parked out front," he continued. "Can I help with your bag?"

He grabbed the handle of her suitcase, lifting it as if it weighed next to nothing, and headed for the door. But she knew for a fact that the five pairs of shoes she'd packed were like a set of bricks. She maintained a careful distance behind her Prada luggage just in case Brody decided to stop short and trip her up. After what she'd done, she wouldn't blame him.

In the lot, she watched as he secured their bags in the locked and covered bed of his pickup. He went around to the passenger side and held her door open, slamming it once she'd settled into the seat. Then he climbed into the driver's side, secured his belt, and slipped the key into the ignition.

And froze.

"I don't get it." Brody turned to her, his hand still on the key. "Why didn't you tell me last night?"

"If you'd known I was your brother's doctor," she said, meeting his searching gaze, "would you have followed me to the pool?"

"No."

"That's why."

"Was it because of the kid on the mountain? Was this your shrink's way of helping me? Did you think I needed last night?"

"I wanted to help you," she said evenly. "And I didn't lie about working in the ER, Brody. I did a long, painful rotation during my residency. But that's not why I went back to your room. Desire is a powerful emotion."

He slid her a glance as if he didn't quite buy that her explanation ended there. But she wasn't about to tell him she'd had a crush on him in high school, or that she remembered him as the white knight of shoes.

"I know," he said.

They rode in silence as he merged onto the highway leading to the Willamette Valley and Independence Falls. "You said you were from here. Did you go to high school in Independence Falls?"

She heard the implied question—*Who the hell are you?*—and knew she owed him an explanation. As much as she wanted him to suddenly remember her from high school and admitting that, oh yeah, he'd noticed her once upon a time, Brody deserved the truth.

"I was a year behind you in school," she explained.

"Do your parents still live here?" he demanded.

"No."

"Independence Falls isn't New York City, I must have known them," he said, frustration filling his tone.

"My mother died when I was five. A drunk-driving accident. She was the drunk. And she was all I had," Kat said, keeping her tone calm and collected while she recited the facts. "She'd moved to Oregon to work in one of the mills not long before the accident. We didn't have family and friends in the area. Or anywhere, really. My father was never part of the picture. Last I knew he was still incarcerated. He shot his dealer when I was a baby, according to my social worker. I grew up in foster care, mostly placed with families on the outskirts of town."

The section of Independence Falls where practically everyone struggled to make ends meet. The neighborhoods where people needed the money the state offered for taking in a foster child.

He stole another glance as if still trying to place her.

"I got braces after medical school and dyed my hair," she said, meeting his searching gaze.

His eyes widened with shock and he turned back to the road. "I remember you now. Your picture was in the paper when you left for Harvard. Not a lot of kids from around here go to an Ivy League school."

And not many who'd grown up moving from house to house with all of their possessions in a black industrial-strength garbage bag.

"I did well on my SATs. And spending twelve years with ten different foster families gave me a lot to write about in my essays," she said, clinging tight to a trace of humor.

"Now you work with one of the leading neurologists in the country," he said.

"I went to John Hopkins for medical school and obtained my Ph.D. from there as well." She needed to erase any doubts about her clinical trial. Regardless of his feelings toward her, the course of treatment she'd designed with Dr. Westbury was his brother's best option.

"Dr. Westbury and I came up with this therapy together," she continued. "She's been researching short-term memory loss resulting from traumatic brain injuries for two decades. Together we formed a plan that treats the whole patient, looking for signs of depression, working through those feelings, while at the same time trying to retrain the memory."

"I read the paperwork," he said. "And to be honest, you're our last hope, which is why I would never have invited you up to my room if I'd know you would be working with Josh."

She looked out the window, guilt washing over her as the outskirts of the city disappeared, replaced by farmland. This was the Oregon she remembered. The land of tall trees, timber mills, small towns, and emotions she'd hoped to leave buried in her past.

"Last night spun out of control," she said. "But it won't happen again."

"No," he said firmly. "It won't."

"I also need you to trust that I can help your brother. I swore when I left that I'd never set foot in Independence

Falls again, but I'm here now for one reason—to treat Josh."

"You don't have any ties here? You didn't keep in touch with your foster parents?"

"The people who sent me packing the minute their obligation to keep me expired? No, we don't send Christmas cards. Especially the families from when I was in high school. I didn't exactly make life easy for them. Most made it pretty clear in return that they didn't want to see me again after the social worker came to pick me up and take me to the next house."

She focused on the cows grazing in the field beside the road. "I guess family just isn't my thing."

KAT'S WORDS ECHOED in his head as he put on his blinker and took the exit marked Independence Falls. Not her thing? Family defined his life. When his mother walked out on them not long after his dad returned from serving overseas, Brody had stepped up. He'd helped his father with everything from laundry to figuring out how to tame his little sister's curls so Katie didn't go school looking like a wild animal.

When his dad died seven years ago, he'd done everything he could to make sure his siblings understood that family came first in his life. He'd go to his grave before he let them down.

But there was a world of difference between his childhood in Independence Falls and Kat's experience. He remembered her picture running in the paper when she left for college. But his memories of her didn't end there. In high school, he'd run into her in the art room when he went back to pick up an assignment. And he'd stay to help fix her shoes.

He remembered the exact moment he realized that she'd labeled them her "lucky shoes" because they were her only shoes. Brody and his siblings hadn't had much while growing up, but their father worked hard to make sure they could afford clothes and sneakers.

He'd gone home from school that day and asked his dad if his mother had left behind a pair of sneakers. And he could still remember his dad's words.

If she asked you not to tell anyone and you show up with a pair of beat-up old shoes that probably won't fit—your mom had boats for feet—how do you think that will make her feel? Keep her confidence, Brody. And let the girl keep her pride.

A few days later he saw her walking in the halls and waved. Glancing down, he spotted new shoes on her feet. Somehow, his father had found a way to get her a new pair of sneakers without hurting her pride.

"Brody, I know you're close with your brothers," Kat said, drawing him back to the present and the fact that the beautiful doctor riding shotgun didn't need his pity now, years later. "But I think it would be best if we didn't share the details of last night with your siblings."

"We're close, but not the close," Brody said. "What happened last night stays between us. You have my word."

"Thank you," Kat said. "I appreciate your discretion."

He nodded, his teeth grinding together. Hell would

freeze over before he told his siblings he'd bound Josh's doctor with her own clothes.

"But Brody?"

He stole a quick glance at her. "Yeah?"

"For what it's worth," she said, her voice a low rumble. "I liked it. It can't happen again. But I don't want you to feel shy about sharing your fantasies."

Her words went straight to his groin. Despite being somewhat influenced by his brain, his lower half didn't seem to care that he couldn't touch her again. Not while she was treating Josh.

Add in the fact that she'd been passed from family to family as a kid and it would be flat out wrong to offer anything—like another night of kinky sex—that suggested he was using her. Dr. Katherine Arnold might as well have been walking around with a sign over her head that read: Brody Summers, Don't Even Think About It.

But logic couldn't shake the image of Kat against the door, her hands bound behind her back, screaming his name.

He shouldn't feel a damn thing for her after the way she'd left out the bit about being the most complicated woman he could possibly find for a night of no-holds-barred sex. Still, the parts of him that responded to that mental flashback felt a whole helluva lot. Maybe it was the fact that she liked being tied up with her own clothes while he tasted her. Or maybe it was the memories of Kat as a girl and her damn shoes.

He could picture her sitting at that art table in clothes

that didn't fit quite right. And as a teenager, he'd taken a strong interest in the girls who wore tight clothes. Even before he could touch, he had to admit he liked to look at a woman's curves.

Breasts weren't the only feature that drew him in. Not anymore. He had a soft spot for people who needed him. The accomplished doctor might not want him. But the girl he remembered? The one who'd traveled through life alone for too long? She might.

Brody pressed on the brake before making a right onto the road into town. He was pretty damn certain that was his dick trying to reason with his common sense. If she'd needed a friend—or more—back when she called this place home, she didn't now.

Out of the corner of his eye he saw her studying the buildings as they hit the outskirts of Main Street. "Bring back memories?"

"Yes."

They drove past the police station, town hall, and the best and only pizza place in town, A Slice of Independence. "Are you hungry? I can stop if you want to pick something up."

"No thank you. I can walk into town later, once I'm settled at the hotel," she said.

"It's a bit of a hike. Are you sure you don't want to rent a car? Or you could borrow one of our trucks. Josh has only driven his once since he moved back home. I'd like to keep it that way for a while longer."

She shook her head. "I have my license, but it's been a year or two since I was behind the wheel. Much longer since I drove a stick. Most of the time, I use a car service when visiting patients."

"Independence Falls doesn't have a taxi company. But between myself and my brother and sister, we can get you where you need to go."

"Thank you. If it is OK with you, I'd like to meet Josh before we stop at the hotel."

"Good. He's eager to get started. And if it is all right with you, we all want to be there for the first meeting."

"Of course. I want you and your siblings involved from the start. I only have two weeks to work with him and his caregivers before I return to Manhattan."

One more item for the list of reasons he couldn't touch her. She was already counting down the days until she returned to New York City.

Chapter 7

_____

KAT SAT AT the Summers family kitchen table, a piece of furniture Brody had handcrafted using downed trees on the property. Two of the Summers siblings had offered that fact when she'd run her hand over the smooth surface, admiring the woodwork. Josh sat at the far end, armed with a notebook and pen, flanked by his siblings.

"We'll begin with a series of information processing tests," Kat explained, focusing on her patient. She glanced down at the chart in front of her. "Your records show that you have already begun taking the antidepressant, and we'll continue with the medication."

"Even if it's not working?" Chad asked. He might have looked like his big brother, Brody, but Chad's default expression was warm and charming.

"Josh, do you feel it is helping?" she asked. She'd agreed to let the family sit in while she discussed her plans because she needed their help executing aspects of

Josh's treatment. But at the end of the day, she was here for Josh.

Brody shifted in his chair. "I believe last night was a clear signal the drug isn't doing enough."

Josh glanced down at his notebook and then up at Brody. "Do you only get laid when you're feeling down, bro? That sure explains a lot."

Like last night, she thought. At the hotel.

Tension radiated off the man sitting next to her. "This isn't about me."

"The medication can only do so much on its own," Kat said, seeking to regain control of the conversation before her mind wandered into the why-did-Brody-take-me-to-his-room last night territory. She had a feeling the answer to that question was simple: sometimes a person simply wanted.

And sometimes the wanting didn't fade in the light of day. She'd expected it to dissipate when they hit the Independence Falls town line. This place didn't exactly inspire happy thoughts. But Brody and the memory of how he'd looked at her last night, like he wanted to possess every inch of her . . . that image took happy thoughts to a sinfully delicious new level.

And an entirely inappropriate place for her first meeting with Josh.

She drew a deep breath and continued. "While Josh and I work on exercises designed to improve his memory recall—"

"How is your trial different from the things they did at the hospital?" Katie Summers, the fiery redhead, stepped in, her expression wary. "And at the rehab facility? The last doctor we brought in had him playing all kinds of memory games."

"My colleague and I developed a course of treatment that takes everyday tasks, things that involve completing steps in a particular sequence, actions that take stimuli from the external environment, and process that stimuli into coherent thought," she explained. "Baking is one activity that is working well for us."

"Doc, you think that if I make a cake my memory will come back?" Josh said, in a tone that clearly labeled her as crazy.

"Not at first, but over time it is one of the things that might help." She glanced around the table. "Keeping a consistent environment is also important."

"So Brody can't fire Megan, huh?" Josh said.

"I think you might need to discuss your relationship with your caregiver. If she becomes more of a girlfriend, you may want to hire someone else. I'm not saying she can't fulfill both roles, but it presents a conflict."

"One he doesn't need right now," Brody said.

She nodded, meeting his serious gaze. Brody had heard her words and applied them to their situation. But a few nights of kinky sex didn't have to be complicated. Not for Josh, or for his reserved-in-public/wild-in-the-bedroom big brother.

No, don't go there! You can't get involved, a little voice shouted in her head. She was here to focus on her job.

"I'm writing that down. Doctor green-lighted sex." Josh glanced up the table at Brody. "Maybe you should ask the doctor if she has any advice for you, bro? Ways to spice up your personal life."

"Josh," his sister said, her tone somewhere between teasing and serious. "Leave Brody alone. He's only trying to help."

"I would be happy to sit down with your brother and talk through his feelings," Kat said. Her teasing words might come back to haunt her, but she couldn't help poking the man who looked like he might shatter from tension. "But I doubt your big brother needs my advice."

Josh let out a bark of laughter. "I like you, Dr. Arnold. So, when do we make our first cake?"

AN HOUR LATER, seated in the cab of Brody's truck as they sped down the two-lane country roads, Kat gave the first meeting with Josh a mental V for victory. Brody's little brother liked her. That would make presenting him with challenging and sometimes frustrating tasks much easier. And yes, she felt a tiny bit bad that those words—*I like you, Dr. Arnold*—had come at Brody's expense. Judging from his stony expression, Brody wasn't ready to do cartwheels over her progress.

"For the record, I never mentioned last night," she said.

"Thank you." He bit out the words as if still struggling to keep his frustration under lock and key.

"And I meant what I said, I'm happy to listen if you need someone to talk to," she added.

"I don't need a shrink," he said. "Last night didn't

happen because I'd hit a breaking point or was over-whelmed with relief."

"Are you sure?" she asked softly, even though the answer might cut open a fresh wound. And right now, driving through this town, she didn't need anything else pulling at her defenses.

"I took one look at your legs and I wanted to taste every inch of you," he growled. "Kat, I can't escape the mental picture of you up against that door. And, right now, driving past Mrs. Henry's goat farm, your panties are burning a freaking hole in my pocket."

"You found my underwear?" A smile formed on her lips. Knowing this man wanted her—not an escape from the stress bearing down on him—spoke to a part of her brain she'd tried to intentionally disconnect in college and medical school. The part that made her draw hearts in her high school notebook around the words *Brody & Kat*.

"Yeah."

"Planning to return them?"

He hit the break and turned the wheel, bringing the truck to a dead stop on the side of the two-lane road. Guiding the stick into Park with near-frantic move-ments, Brody lifted his hips and withdrew the thong from his pocket.

"Here." His gaze locked with hers as he held out the forgotten panties.

Without looking away, she plucked them from his hand, her fingers brushing his, sending electric pulses racing through her. Her body begged to even the orgasm count right here in the front seat of his truck.

"Thank you." She ran her tongue over her lips, drawing his attention. Every inch of her body screamed *Kiss me, take me, now.* "Brody—"

"I can't." Shifting in his seat—it didn't take a series of anatomy lectures from medical school to recognize the fact that this man was very turned on—Brody put the truck in Drive. "You're my brother's doctor," he added.

"That's right. Josh's. Not yours," she said as he merged onto the road. "What's between us has nothing to do with your brother's treatment. You have my word on that."

He shook his head. "It's too complicated."

"I know," she admitted. "But it might be fun."

And a welcome distraction from unwanted memories.

Glancing out the window, she saw the familiar sights of Main Street. They were close to the hotel now. She could use the distraction to make some new memories there. He could take control, whisper his fantasies in her ear—anything to keep her focused on the here and now.

"Just think about it, Brody," she added, her gaze focused on the Falls Hotel as they pulled into the parking lot. "Please."

SITTING NEXT TO Dr. Katherine Arnold was like steering a semi hauling a load of logs through an unexpected whiteout. He had no clue what she would do or say next. He'd fought the urge to yell "What the hell" when she'd hinted at his sex life while seated at his kitchen table. He wanted to rein her in, to fight for control even though he couldn't for the life of him anticipate what would come out of her mouth next.

Then she'd said please, and he wanted to be the one to grant her every wish, to hell with consequences. But he'd already played that card, letting desire win, and look where it landed him.

"I'll think about it," he said, even though he couldn't shake the feeling that another night with Kat wasn't the right move. "But first let's get you settled."

Then he needed to haul ass back home, shower, shave, and dress for Eric Moore's wedding to Georgia Trulane.

He parked by the front entrance, stepped down from the truck and went around to get her bag. Kat took the handle but didn't move to the hotel entrance. Staring straight ahead, her lips sank into a frown.

"I know it's not the Ritz," he said. "But the Falls Hotel is the only option in town."

Unless he offered her the studio apartment over his barn. His brothers, and sometimes his little sister, used it as a place to take their dates. He'd done the same once or twice when he didn't feel like subjecting a girlfriend to his family. But now Chad spent most of his time at Lena's apartment, Katie had moved in with Liam, and Josh, well up until last night he'd been off the market. But the thought of having Kat so close, teasing him at every turn—that thought tied him in knots.

"The hotel is clean and comfortable," he said. "But I doubt it has changed much since you lived here. Same

1980s interior. Not that you had any reason to come here as a kid."

"I don't need fancy." Kat tightened her grip on her suitcase handle, but she didn't step forward. "And I've been inside before."

"Prom?"

She shook her head. "I didn't go to prom. When I was seven, my social worker took me to an adoption event held in the hotel lobby. Prospective families from the area who might be willing to adopt an older child."

Her voice trembled as if she'd left her bold, self-assured tone in his truck. One look at her stricken expression and he felt as if he'd been punched in the gut. The seductive woman, the one who'd faced him head-on when revealing her true reasons for traveling to Oregon, had vanished. In her place stood a person who looked as if she'd been delivered to the doorstep of a nightmare.

"Didn't go well, huh?" he said, trying to picture her as a grade-school child. He barely remembered her from high school, and his mind couldn't make the jump.

"I brought my science fair project," she said. "You remember those trifold boards?"

"Yeah. My dad took us to the hardware store to pick them up around science fair time each year," he said, unsure how the poster related to the fact that her feet were glued to the white line dividing his parking space from the empty one beside his truck.

"My second grade teacher made sure I had one that year. My project was about the solar system. For a while

I thought I wanted to be an astronaut. I presented it to every family. I wanted to show them I was smart. But . . ."

She shrugged, forcing a smile. "No one called about me. I guess they didn't like my hypothesis. Funny thing is, I can't even remember what I was trying to prove."

"You don't have to laugh it off," he said.

"It was a long time ago. I can see the humor now."

And he could still see the heartache.

Brody fought the urge to wrap her in his arms and hold her tight. One glance at Kat told him a porcupine would be more receptive to a hug right now. But damn it, he wanted to offer her something. He understood childhood sorrow and despair. When his mother left, he'd wondered why she hadn't wanted him and his siblings. But he had chalked it up to something being wrong with his mom, and he'd focused on the people who wanted him. His brothers. His sister. His father. He'd never had to prove he was worthy of a family. Not to them.

At seven years old, Kat had walked into that hotel alone and believing no one wanted her, and she'd left with confirmation. Maybe he couldn't hug her, but he had to do something.

"We have a studio apartment over the barn," he said. "You can't walk to town, but you'd be close to Josh."

"Thank you, but I'll be fine at the hotel," she said, stepping off the white line. "I'd forgotten all about that day until we pulled into the lot."

Yeah, that was a big fat lie.

"Kat, do you have plans tonight?"

He couldn't stand the thought of her alone in that hotel surrounded by the memory of her seven-year-old self determined to prove her worth and then coming up empty.

Kat glanced over her shoulder, pausing in the space marked for a car. "I was planning to catch up on work. And update Dr. Westbury on my first meeting with Josh."

"Give Dr. Westbury another day to recover from surgery," he said. "It's your first night back. And Eric Moore is getting married up at Willamette Valley Vineyards. He's younger than us, but you might remember him. Georgia, Eric's bride, reserved a spot for Josh, but he's been clear he doesn't want to go. You might see some familiar faces."

"You're inviting me to a wedding?" Her green eyes widened. "That's your idea of having some fun together?"

No, he was still on the fence about more "fun." But she could label it whatever she wanted as long as she said yes. "For tonight, yeah it is."

Kat frowned. "I didn't pack a dress."

He glanced down at her suitcase. From where he was standing, it looked as if she'd packed half her closet. Or maybe she'd only brought the short skirts and fancy underwear.

"Wear whatever you want," he said, pushing aside his mental wish list of Things in Kat's Bag. "According to my sister—she is the maid-of-honor—Georgia is so focused on her dress that she doesn't care what the guests wear."

"I can't crash some poor girl's wedding," Kat protested. "She doesn't know me."

"Trust me, Kat. It will be fine." His sister had been hounding him to bring a date, and Katie had roped Georgia into her cause. The bride would be thrilled he'd chosen a last minute plus one. And Eric didn't care if all the guests bailed as long as he got to marry Georgia.

"I'll pick you up at five," he called over his shoulder as he headed for his truck. He climbed in and closed the door before she could object again. Watching her wheel her fancy suitcase into the hotel, each step betraying her irritation, he knew he'd made the right call by inviting her.

For one night, he wanted Kat to feel like she was a part of Independence Falls. He wanted to give her a new reason to like this place. And yeah, he could tell himself he was doing it for Josh, to make his brother's doctor feel at home while treating him. But he knew that was a lie.

He was doing this for her. Wild, sexy Kat had gotten under his skin last night. And now he couldn't shake the feeling that she was his. Maybe he couldn't tie her to his bed and make her scream his name, but he could look out for her. He could be the one person in this town that she could count on to make sure that returning home didn't hurt quite so much.

Chapter 8

NUMBERS NEVER LIED. Emotions on the other hand were like smoke screens. Hopes rose only to be crushed. And love remained an elusive, indefinable thing always out of her grasp. But the numbers, the cold hard facts, were always there for her. From the SATs to the MCATs, they shaped her world.

"There are only twenty people here," she whispered, scanning the four rows of white plastic chairs. The intimate seating area faced a white wooden arbor lined with colorful wildflowers. Beyond the spot where the bride and groom would say their vows, fields of grape vines sloped up and down hills. The Cascade Mountains were a backdrop to the picture-perfect scene. Still snowcapped on a warm April day, the peaks were breathtakingly beautiful, even to a confirmed city girl who loved her skyscrapers.

Either the bride had blown her budget on the location and needed to cut the guest list by one hundred, or she'd planned a small wedding. After googling multimillionaire Eric Moore in her hotel room, Kat had a feeling it was option B.

"The groom runs the largest timber operation in the Pacific Northwest and he only invited twenty guests?" she said, running her hands over the sheer black pleated top layer to her skirt. Beneath the see-through fabric, the nude pencil skirt hugged her curves. She'd paired the off-the-runway piece with a bright blue silk blouse for a pop of vibrant color. The simple fact that she hadn't packed a dress appropriate for a wedding demanded the skirt/shirt combination.

Glancing around at the other guests, she could have worn a simple shift and sweater. Most of the women had selected dresses for the occasion. One or two fit the label cocktail attire. The rest reminded Kat of Sunday services in Independence Falls. The family she'd lived with when she was eleven had taken her every week. And a couple of the outfits here tonight looked as if they dated back to that era. The men wore jackets, though one guest seated across the aisle had paired his sports coat with a Moore Timber T-shirt, jeans, and cowboy boots.

"Georgia recently returned from Afghanistan," Brody said, leaning close and keeping his voice low. "She's out of the army now, but large crowds make her nervous. She decided to keep the wedding to friends, a few coworkers, and family."

The bride was a veteran with PTSD? That had to top the list of weddings *not* to crash.

"I shouldn't be here," Kat said.

Brody took her hand as if he thought she might run. It was tempting, but the last thing Kat wanted to do was startle the bride by racing away from her wedding ceremony.

Chad Summers claimed the empty seat on her right, the one bordering the pathway between the chairs. He smiled at her, his brown eyes brimming with mischief. "I heard a rumor that you'd decided to bring a date," he said to his brother. "I didn't realize it was the new doctor."

"I'm not his date," Kat said quickly, pulling her hand free from Brody's hold. "I was tricked into crashing."

Chad's eyebrows shot up. "By my big brother?"

"How's Lena?" Brody demanded, in what she suspected was an attempt to shut down his brother's curiosity.

Chad smiled at the woman's name. "Ready to blaze a path down the aisle. She was getting Hero prepared to do his part when I left. He's one good-looking flower dog."

Traditional wedding music ended the conversation. The groom appeared at the front in a charcoal three-piece suit. Beside him stood an equally attractive gentleman. She didn't recognize either one—though she guessed Mr. Three-Piece Suit was Eric Moore. Still, one look around the small wedding and Kat had to admit the single, female population of Manhattan might flock to small-town Oregon if they realized the abundance of drool-worthy men.

Abandoning any hope of escaping this friends and family event, Kat turned her attention to the white runner leading to the arbor. A small boy, about three or four, appeared. He clutched a pillow with two rings tied to the top in one hand and a small plastic sheep in the other. Dropping the pillow, he raced to the front, heading straight for the groom.

"Nate, the rings!" an older woman, possibly the bride or groom's mother, called to the child.

Eyes wide with surprise, the young ring bearer raced back, discarded the toy sheep, picked up the pillow and returned to the front.

The bridal procession continued with a golden retriever carrying a white wicker basket overflowing with rose petals. As the dog trotted toward the arbor, petals tumbled to the white runner. A blond woman who looked as if she belonged on the Fashion Week runway despite her somewhat ordinary tea-length green dress followed close behind. The animal paused by the abandoned sheep and cocked its head as if debating whether to drop the basket and continue on with the toy.

"Don't you dare, Hero," the blond woman murmured, and the retriever obeyed. Katie Summers followed in a matching dress, the green highlighting her red hair.

"My sister's boyfriend is the guy standing beside the groom," Brody said, his voice low. "Liam Trulane. He's also Georgia's brother. They grew up here too."

"One big happy family, huh?" Kat whispered as the music changed and the audience stood.

"We have out moments," Brody murmured, his lips curving up, forming a smile that managed to scream sexy and sweet at the same time. "But for the most part? Yeah, one big family."

Why do I have a feeling your worst moments together surpass my best memory of "having a family"?

Because even at their worst, they had each other.

Turning to the aisle, Kat wondered if she should slip away after the ceremony. She didn't belong here. The connections in her life didn't run deep. Even the ones that scratched the surface—her friends from medical school, her colleagues in New York, her mentor—none of those relationships had roots in this town.

She'd grown up with these people but didn't recognize them. She'd planned to march into town, her look-you-were-wrong-about-me attitude in place. But so far no one remembered her.

The anonymity left her unsettled. And wondering if she'd given her past and this place too much weight.

The bride appeared, her smile wide and her brown eyes brimming with excitement. Georgia moved with slow, measured steps as if it took all of her self-restraint not to race to the arbor and greet her groom. The simple ivory strapless dress flowed effortlessly around her. It was a classic, elegant choice, apart from the black lace sash wrapped around her waist. The sash, a modern twist that set the gown apart, formed a big bow at the back.

Watching this woman, a virtual stranger who'd fought in a war, survived, and struggled with the aftereffects, head for her groom, the number of people present faded into the background and emotion took over. And so what if they didn't remember her? This was Georgia's moment.

"Eric, it feels like I've loved you forever," the bride

said, beaming up at her groom. "And then I fell head first *in* love with you. I trust you to always see me and believe in me. And I promise to do the same for you. I can fight the scary bears alone, Eric. But together, as a family—" The bride stole a quick glance at the ring bearer.

"Nate is Eric's nephew," Brody explained in a low voice. "He took the kid in after his parents died."

Kat's gaze snapped to the little boy as an imaginary band squeezed her heart. Joy chased the rush of pain she felt for his loss. He wasn't alone. The child had lost so much, yet gained these people, who were openly declaring their love for one another.

"Together as a family," Georgia continued. "We'll fight the scary bears."

Eric reached out and took her hand. "Always, Georgia. Always."

The ring bearer gave a solemn nod.

"My turn?" Eric said. And then without waiting for confirmation, he began: "I'll keep this short because I'm dying to kiss my beautiful bride."

The audience laughed and Nate scrunched up his nose.

"I always try to do the right thing, make the right choices. And loving you, Georgia? Standing by your side, taking care of you no matter what life throws our way, nothing has ever felt so right. I promise to love you for the rest of my life, trusting in you, believing in you. I'm going to do whatever it takes to make you happy. Always."

Happiness—looking at the bride and groom, Kat believed it was possible. But it had often felt out of place amid these mountains. Still, she had changed, and so had Independence Falls. She didn't have to spend her time here revisiting the unwanted feelings that had descended on her swift and fierce outside the Falls Hotel. She could find new ones, bury the long-held hurts.

And she could choose to spend her brief time here with the football star who'd offered a helping hand once upon a time. Brody Summers was one of the best things this town had to offer, then and certainly now that he'd matured into a man who knew how to use his sinfully perfect body to deliver the world's best orgasms.

Judging from the way he'd pulled over and handed back her panties, he wanted her too.

"Brody," she whispered as the groom kissed his beautiful bride. "Do you dance?"

"It's been a while," he admitted, his gaze fixed on the happy couple.

"I think you proved last night that lack of practice doesn't diminish your ability to perform."

Cheering, music, and the officiant's words, "I now pronounce you man and wife," interrupted. Kat stood, clapping and smiling as the bride and groom raced down the aisle followed by the empty-handed little boy and the golden retriever.

"But I can't dance with you," Brody murmured.

His words took the edge off her happiness. "Then why did you bring me?"

She knew the answer as soon as the words escaped.

Pity. She'd offered a window into her past and Mr. Do-the-Right-Thing had felt sorry for her. Her grade school science project was coming back to haunt her again. But she refused to let it win.

"I thought you'd have fun," he said.

And you couldn't stand the thought of leaving me at the hotel. He'd meant well. She wasn't blind to that fact. But she hated the idea that this man looked at her and saw a dog that had been kicked one too many times. She wasn't a rescue project. Not anymore.

The guests followed the bridal party into the winery's event space. Floor-to-ceiling windows showed tables decorated with simple yet elegant centerpieces, a dance floor, and a long wooden bar lined with wine bottles. But Kat hung back, allowing the invited guests to join the bride and groom.

"I will have fun," she said. "If you dance with me."

Winning a yes from Brody suddenly felt necessary. It had been years since anyone had caught a glimpse beneath the facade she presented to the world. In New York no one looked at her and saw "orphan." No one offered Dr. Katherine Arnold a pity date, not to a wedding or anywhere else.

She stepped into the reception and scanned the crowd. "I could ask that cowboy over there. The one wearing the T-shirt."

"Craig?" Brody's hand moved to her lower back, his finger brushing the outer layer of her skirt. "He's one of Eric's crew chiefs."

"A man who wields a chainsaw can't dance?" she challenged as he guided her toward the bar.

Brody's jaw locked, his hand pressing tight against her back. "I'll do it. I'll dance with you."

TWENTY MINUTES LATER, after the bride and groom completed their first spin around the dance floor, Brody set his beer on the bar and held out his hand. A lively, familiar country song filled the room. He might look like a fool moving to the upbeat tempo, but he couldn't risk a long, slow song that demanded close contact. If he held her body up against his, it wouldn't end there.

"Ready?" he asked.

"You always keep your word, don't you?" Kat placed her wineglass beside his beer and allowed him to lead her to the center of the cleared area.

"If I say I'm going to do something, I do it." He placed one hand on her waist and tried not to think about what her curves looked like free from her fancy clothes.

"Hmmm," she murmured, moving closer, ignoring his attempt to keep her body from pressing up against his. "I'm tempted to wiggle a naughty promise out of you."

Brody frowned. "I don't think this is the time or place."

Her hand moved up his shoulder to where his shirt collar stopped. Her fingertips teased the bare skin. "I'm sure they have a quiet storage room. From what I recall, you don't need much, just a solid door, maybe a wall for support."

"I'm not sure about that." He stepped back and spun her in a tight circle. The see-through layer of her skirt lifted, practically begging him to haul her off the dance floor. That damn fabric had taunted him from the moment he'd spotted her in the hotel parking lot, striding toward his truck. Part of him wanted to disappear beneath it, and yeah, a solid door in a secluded storage room would work for that. But that sure as heck wasn't why he'd brought her.

"Bump into any old friends?" he asked as her body pressed close again.

"No."

Kat drew away, stopping short of trying to solicit a promise, naughty or nice, from him. But it didn't change the fact that regret grabbed him by the balls the minute she backed off. His body—currently at war with his mind—flat-out desired her.

"But I'm glad you invited me. It was a beautiful wedding. And I like to dance." She leaned in close, rising up on her tiptoes, her lips close to his ear. "Spin me again, Brody."

He did as she asked, twirling her around. The transparent top layer of her skirt lifted again. The nude-colored bottom layer offered the illusion that she was naked underneath. Maybe she was beneath the skirt.

His body reacted to the image as he drew her back into his arms. The accomplished doctor wouldn't attend a wedding without her panties. Either way, he shouldn't be thinking about her underwear.

The music ended and he released her. "I'm going to grab another beer. Want anything?"

"No thanks." She shook her head. "I need a moment to freshen up. And find that storage room."

She winked at him, turned and walked off the dance floor. His eyes followed every movement of her flowing skirt. Right or wrong, he couldn't help wanting her.

The next song started and he headed for the keg.

"Are you sure you picked up the right doctor?" his brother said.

Brody glanced up from the self-service barrel of local brew. "She's filling in for Dr. Westbury."

"You didn't just offer a ride to the first sexy blonde you saw and hope she had a few letters after her name like MD and Ph.D.?" Chad said.

"Shouldn't you be focused on your own blonde?" Brody waved his hand, gesturing to where Lena was dancing with her dog on the edge of the dance floor.

"I'm serious, Brody. I know Josh likes her, but she's planning on teaching him how to bake. I didn't go to medical school, but how is mixing sugar and butter going to help?"

"She's the right doctor," he said, hoping that would end the discussion. "And you're the one who shoved the information about this clinical trial under my nose last month. Whatever they are doing, it's working. Three former NFL players have sought Dr. Westbury out after suffering multiple concussions."

"True," Chad admitted. "Then mind telling me why the hell you brought her here?"

Brody turned to face his brother, his back to the party. "I couldn't leave her alone in the hotel for the night. You probably don't remember her, but before Kat moved to New York and became a top doctor, she was a foster kid who bounced around from home to home."

"Kat, huh? So you brought her as your date to, what, fix the past?" Chad said, raising his drink to his lips.

"It's not a date."

"I saw you out there, dancing with her. If you plan on holding all of Josh's caregivers close during a country love song, you're going to have to fight the kid for Megan. Maybe he can't remember what they did together last night, but he sure as shit liked what he read in his notebook this morning."

"Guys, I have nothing against your brother's intimate relationship with his caregiver." Kat's voice cut in, the low throaty quality reminding him that dancing with her had nothing to do with rescuing Kat from a lonely night in the hotel room. Kat had looked at Craig, who by all accounts was a decent guy, and a great crew chief, and Brody had wanted to claim possession of her. "But you," she continued, poking the center of Brody's chest with her index finger, "should probably stay away."

Chad chuckled. "You know, Doctor, I think you might be good for him."

"I've treated enough patients with traumatic brain injuries to know that depression can play a serious role in their recovery," she said.

"Not Josh." His brother shook his head. "You're good for Brody."

Chad winked at them before walking away to join his girl and her dancing golden retriever. When his brother was out of earshot, Brody turned to face Kat. Fire and determination shone in her green eyes and he knew she'd overheard too much.

"Kat—"

"Come with me." She took his free hand, leading him past the bar and into the hallway connecting the reception to the rest of the winery.

"Where are we going?" he demanded as she made a sharp right turn, leading him down a narrow staircase into the winery's underbelly.

"Sweet of you to worry about my past. To take pity on me and bring me as your date. And once you got me here, to think of my happiness and make sure I have a good time." A spark of fury echoed in her low voice, bouncing off the stairwell walls. "But you saw to my happiness last night. Twice. Now it's my turn to see to yours."

Chapter 9

KAT SPUN ON her heels and faced the six-foot-plus towering wall of muscle hidden beneath a suit. Surrounded by wine barrels in the dimly lit storage room, she reached for his tie, drawing him close.

His hands went to her hips, but he didn't push her away. "Kat, I shouldn't have told my brother about your past. I couldn't stand the thought of you alone in that hotel room. What kind of ass would hear your story and not feel for the child who grew up like you did? But this isn't a pity date. That's not what I see when I look at you now."

"What do you see?" she demanded, focusing on the knot in his tie. She needed to hear him say the words, to admit that he wanted her here.

"A beautiful, smart woman who dressed to drive me crazy." His hands ran up and down her hips, bunching the see-through top layer. "While we were dancing I couldn't stop thinking about your skirt." He lowered his mouth to her neck, brushing his lips over her skin. "And what's beneath it."

"What if I told you I'm not wearing any underwear?"

Brody growled against her neck, his grip tightening on her hips. "Show me."

"I can't." She broke free from his hold, taking his undone tie with her. Standing just out of arm's reach, her gaze locked with his. "Because when I look at you, I see a man who is holding onto his control by a thread. A man who remembers exactly where we left off last night. Tonight's my turn to take care of you."

"Kat, if you think last night was about seeing to your happiness, you don't know a damn thing about what makes me happy. Feeling your hips bucking wild and out of control against my face, seeing you tied up, waiting for me to take you there—" He took a step forward, the dark, out-of-control gleam in his eyes suggesting he might pounce.

He reached for her and she danced out of his grasp. "Do you want to hear my fantasy?" she said. "I want to push you past reasonable, to drive you out of control."

He let out a rough laugh. "You've done that."

"I'm not finished." Tossing his tie aside, she put her hands on his chest and backed him up against a barrel. "I've dreamed about what you would feel like."

She left out the "for years" part. Her fingers went to work on his buttons, quickly stripping off his shirt, unveiling the hard contours she'd wanted to explore last night by the pool. So different from the boy she'd know in high school. But she preferred the man.

"I've dreamed about kissing you, claiming you with my mouth."

"Kat—"

"Every inch." She touched her lips to his chest, brushing soft kisses over the body that surpassed her fantasies. In New York she'd dated men who spent hours in the gym fine-tuning their pecs and sculpting their six-packs. They looked like wimps next to Brody Summers.

"Do you work out?" she murmured before flicking her tongue over his nipple.

"No," he said, his voice a low rumble. "I work."

"Saving others looks good on you." She ran her hands over his taunt abdomen. Releasing his belt, she moved on to his pants. Her fingers teased the elastic band on his underwear, slipping beneath. The pad of her thumb brushed his cock. "But I don't need to be rescued."

His hand captured her wrist. "Kat—"

"Admit it, you want me." She pulled free from his hold. Drawing his suit pants and boxers down over his hips, she sank to the ground. Tilting her head back as her hand wrapped around him, stroking from the base to the tip and down, she stared up into his dark brown eyes. She searched for a sign of sympathy. And came up empty. Thank goodness.

She turned her attention to his long, thick length. "If I'd known what you were hiding behind your boxers last night, I would have insisted on having a turn." Her tongue swirled around the head of his cock. "I'm taking one now."

"Jesus." His voice was a low growl seemingly at odds with his Mr. Do-the-Right-Thing reputation. "Yes, I want you."

Lips hovering close, she glanced up at him again. His fingers gripped the upright barrel at his back. His hips thrust toward her hand, demanding more from each stroke. The look in his eyes bordered on feral.

"Tell me what you see when you look at me now," she demanded. The thought that this man, who appeared as if he wanted to devour her, might let sympathy seep back in . . . She wanted to banish the word pity from his vocabulary forever.

"Right now I can't see past your lips." The urgent need in his tone confirmed his words. "Your mouth."

"Good answer," she murmured, wrapping her lips around him. Her tongue stroked him as her mouth ran up and down. His hips bucked forward, setting a frantic rhythm. He wasn't holding back. Not anymore.

"Unbutton your blouse," he said. "Let me see more."

Maintaining a hold on his cock with one hand, her fingers rising up to meet her mouth with each thrust of his hips, she obeyed. He let out a low growl when she reached the last button and ran her hand up over her skin, drawing the shirt away from her breasts. Her fingers danced over the lacy edge where the fabric of her bra met skin.

"When I look at you, I remember how you taste." His voice was a low, steady growl. The sound teased her body, his words taking the place of his hands. "The moment you walked out of the hotel, I wanted to strip off the layers of your skirt. You want to hear me say the words? I want you. From the minute you left my room last night, I've wanted you."

His hips moved faster, demanding more. She drew the cups of her bra down beneath her breasts. His growl of appreciation offered an A for effort.

"I never lose control, but I look at you and—"

She rewarded his wild abandon by pinching her nipple, drawing it out, letting him watch as she drove her own desire.

"Ah hell, Kat. The things I want from you . . ." A low groan replaced words.

"Hold tight to those thoughts," she ordered, her hand working up and down his length. "Close your eyes and let them play out. Every time you look at me, I want you to remember those wild scenes. And then I want you to show me."

BRODY OBEYED, CLOSING his eyes as she reclaimed his cock. The feel of her lips sucking hard, drawing him in, her tongue pushing him closer—he didn't need to imagine Kat stripped naked and lying on his bed to make him explode. But that didn't stop the fantasy reel.

In his bed—ah hell, he wanted her there, naked and waiting for him. He imagined sinking into her, taking her in a way that had nothing to do with careful restraint.

His hips bucked against her mouth. He fought the

urge to run his fingers through her long hair and hold her head.

"I want you, Kat." He opened his eyes and looked down at her. If she needed to hear those words, needed him at admit that desire and lust overrode his brain when it came to her, he'd give her those words over and over. "I want you."

Her breasts bounced as her mouth lifted up and down. Perched over the cups of her bra, her nipples begged for attention. And he couldn't resist. Releasing one hand from the barrel, he reached out and brushed her nipple. He felt the vibration of her moan against his cock.

"Fuck." He bit off the word, the sound of her desire pushing him over the edge. He tried to pull away from her mouth as the climax took hold. But she held tight, refusing to release him. She took everything he had and still left him wanting more—wanting her. When she finally drew back, offering him a wicked grin, he wondered if wanting was the right word. Right now, staring at her lips swollen from sucking him off, need took a firm hold of him. It had nothing to do with her past or the reasons why she'd returned to Independence Falls.

Stepping out of his dress shoes, he shed the rest of his clothes. She tracked his movements. Rocking back on her heels, he thought for a moment she might stand, make her excuses and leave him with an unfulfilled need for more. But they'd come this far. He wasn't going to let her walk away before he heard her call out his name as she came.

"My turn," he said, extending his hand, drawing her up from the floor.

"We'll miss the buffet," she teased.

Wrapping his hands around her waist beneath her open shirt, he guided her until the back of her calves touched a barrel lying on its side. Gently, he lowered her down, positioning her bottom at the curved edge.

"I'll feed you later," he said, dropping to his knees between her spread legs. He tossed the see-through fabric up to her waist. His hands moved to her thighs, drawing the pencil skirt up. And his fingers toyed with the edge of her panties.

"You lied," he murmured, staring at the proof.

"I said 'what if.' I don't crash weddings without underwear," she murmured, the near-breathless sound of her voice betraying her desire. "And don't even think about walking away with those."

"Hmm, I like the idea of you spending the rest of the night without your underwear." He drew the wet slip of lace aside and lowered his mouth, licking until she let out a soft moan.

"I want you, Brody. Inside me," she said. "I don't care if the barrel breaks. Take me in a pool of wine. *Please*."

Brody drew back, his gaze traveling to where her hands moved over her breasts. She might have said please, but she wasn't begging. Kat was issuing an order. And he wanted to comply, but—

"I don't have a condom." He slipped a finger inside and felt her tense around him. Her hips lifted off the barrel, demanding more. He added a second and she arched, her bottom pressing into the barrel's metal-rimmed edge.

"Ouch," she muttered, quickly lifting up.

"We're not breaking out the wine tonight," he said, slipping his fingers out. Rising up on his knees, he wrapped his hands around her waist and took her with him as he moved to the floor. Letting go, he laid down on his back. "Hold your skirt up and kneel over my face."

She followed his instructions, allowing him to draw her panties aside with one hand as he ran his tongue over her. His free hand squeezed her ass, his fingers following the line of her thong. Kat moaned, her hips moving over his mouth, demanding more. He felt her control slip away, her movements driven by a desire to get there, to reach the peak of pleasure.

She cried out and her body fell forward, her hands pressing into the cellar floor above his head. Her skirt buried his face as she came and he didn't give a damn.

Her thighs trembled as the orgasm swept over her and then receded. Brody reached for her waist, drawing her away from his mouth. Sliding down his torso, she collapsed on his chest, her breathing erratic.

Overhead, he heard the DJ calling the guests up to their seats for the best man's speech. The shuffle of shoes on hardwood drowned out the rest of the announcement.

Sitting up, the fact that he was naked on the cellar floor at his friend's wedding sank in. He glanced at the woman who'd delivered him to this place—this moment—his mind so overrun with wanting her he didn't care where they were.

Kat smoothened her hands over her skirt. "I'll go up first."

"They're going to figure it out." He reached for his clothes. "I'm sorry—"

"For letting me drag you away from the reception?" She shook her head. "That wasn't your fault. If you want to apologize for something, tell me you're sorry you didn't bring a condom."

He let out a laugh as he secured his pants. "I am."

"I forgive you. But next time be more prepared."

She turned and headed for the stairs.

Next time? There wouldn't be a "next time." Hell, he shouldn't have followed her down here, knowing the need to have her would override everything else. The more he learned about Dr. Katherine Arnold, from the childhood that had left her feeling unwanted to the fact that she hated pity, he knew she deserved someone who would go all in for her. But he wasn't in a position to be that man beyond the bedroom walls.

You haven't taken her to bed yet. You just buried your face between her legs on the floor of a wine cellar.

"Kat," he called.

She paused, glancing back at him. Her right hand maintained a firm grip on the banister as she raised an eyebrow.

"As much as I want to take you out and then back to my bed," he said, "there won't be a next time."

"Careful Brody." Her lips formed a wicked smile. "I've never met a challenge I couldn't conquer."

Chapter 10

JOSH SET THE bottle of bourbon beside the vanilla on the counter and turned to face Kat. "What's the next step, Doc?"

She looked up from the chart spread out on the Summers kitchen table, documenting Josh's symptoms from his injury. In addition to his short-term memory loss, her patient had difficulty concentrating and he had headaches. But unlike some of the professional athletes she'd treated, he'd been spared many of the symptoms caused by multiple head injuries. Epilepsy, personality changes—repeated concussions often led to a downward spiral. Treatment and therapy were always an uphill battle. But in Josh's case, they weren't climbing Everest. She had a good feeling that he could recover from this.

"If you can't remember, go back and check the cookbook," she said.

Her patient let out a frustrated grunt. He knew the layout of the kitchen—that part of his memory was still intact—but finding the recipe was another story.

"Doc, I don't know where I put the damn cookbook."

"It's open beside the fridge," she said, offering just enough help to keep the defeated feeling from pushing him to quit—or consult his notebook. If he even remembered it was in his back pocket. "We're making Bourbon Pecan Pie."

"I vote we skip straight to drinking the liquor." Josh picked up the open book. His lips moved as he read the words.

"You picked it."

His brow furrowed. "It says here, we need to place the piecrust in the refrigerator for thirty minutes. Do we even have a piecrust?"

"It's in there," Kat confirmed. "We made it first thing."

"Shit, I don't remember that part."

"Focus on what you're doing now," she said. "What's in your hand?"

Josh glanced at the mixing device. "Doc, I didn't know what this was before I got knocked in the head."

"It's a whisk," she said, keeping her tone calm and even. "Read through the recipe. Find out what comes next."

"Brown sugar, eggs, cream, bourbon." Josh glanced up from the book and focused on the ingredients on the counter. "I was holding the bourbon."

"That's right," Kat said.

"But I don't have a clue about whether I put it in there or not," he said.

"I guess we'll find out when we taste it." Chad Summers waltzed into the room wearing jeans, cowboy boots, and white T-shirt that read, My Hero, My Veteran, My Girl, in big black letters.

"Dip a spoon into what you have so far," Kat suggested as Chad claimed the seat next to her at the table.

"Figuring out if there is bourbon in the batter will help his memory?" Chad murmured.

"Taking stimuli, in this instance, taste from an external source and processing it helps." Or at least that was the hypothesis of their clinical trial.

"It's in there," Josh confirmed. He picked up a bottle and took a swig, then winked at Kat. "For good luck."

Her somewhat unruly patient turned back to the counter and picked up the pecans. Kat watched for a moment before turning her attention to the man beside her. "He remembered that the pecans went in next without having to check."

"So this is a slow and steady wins the race sort of thing?"

"Regaining memory takes time and patience," Kat said. "The best thing you can do for your brother right now is offer support and do what you can to keep his environment the same. I can get him started on the path to recovery, but then he'll need his family and caretakers to help him."

"Oh, I fully intend to give him my support and have a

slice of pie. And we're not letting the nursing student go. We're making it clear to Megan that she has to keep her clothes on while we're paying her. But during her down time . . ." Chad shrugged. "They're adults."

"Good." Kat kept her voice low while her patient worked on his pie. "We're on the same page, then. I think a sexual relationship that extends beyond a handful of encounters might be a good thing for him. It helps with the depression."

"Dr. Arnold, I don't need a medical degree to confirm that sex goes in the plus column. To be honest, I'm not worried about Josh's emotional state when you leave. But Brody's another story."

"He's all grown up too," she said, glancing back at her chart.

"True," Chad said, no longer making an effort to keep his voice low. "But he's always been the serious, responsible one."

Josh let out a snort as he pulled the chilled piecrust from the fridge and consulted the cookbook.

"Which is why we're taking bets on what happened when you two disappeared during Eric and Georgia's wedding reception," Chad said. "My sister thought you might've gotten locked in the bathroom and needed a rescue. Liam went along with her because, well, agreeing with my sister is in his best interest. And saving the day is Brody's specialty. But I saw the way he danced with you and I think it was more of a mutual rescuing."

"I want in," Josh called, pulling the spiral notebook

out of his back pocket. He flipped it open and scanned a page. "Put my money on Brody. He was smiling this morning like he'd gotten lucky last night."

Kat reached for her pen, determined to shift the focus on the conversation. "Josh, you knew to look in your notebook for that detail. That's great."

Josh stuffed the notebook into his jeans pocket. "Don't get too excited, Doc. Brody parted ways with his last serious girlfriend nearly a year ago. I knew if he looked like he'd gotten some action, I'd have written it down. Easier to give him grief later."

"I'm not his girlfriend," she said quickly.

"But you weren't locked in the bathroom waiting to be rescued last night," Chad said.

"I don't need your brother to save me." She turned her attention to the chart. "But in terms of the bet, you'd have to ask Brody."

"I just might to do that." Chad pushed back from the table. "While I'm at it, I'll remind him that you're not his girlfriend. And that you're leaving soon."

"He knows," she said.

Chad placed his palms flat on the table and his smile vanished. "If that fact was front and center in his mind, Brody would never have left the reception last night. My brother goes all in for the people he cares about. And the way he looked at you last night, I'd say you're on that list. Maybe he hasn't woken up to that fact yet, but he will."

The warning rang in her ears as Chad turned to Josh. "Save some pie for me, bro." And then he slipped out the kitchen door and headed for the barn.

"Hey, Doc."

Kat pushed Chad's words away and focused on the man placing a pie into the oven. Fingers crossed it was edible. Most of the other patients in their trial had some prior cooking experience. The inspiration for the study, Maureen from upstate New York, had been a pastry chef before a horseback riding accident temporarily stole her short-term memory. Maureen had given Kat the idea to try cooking as a way to help patients recover their memory. Kat never would have come up with it by herself. Before she'd started working with patients, her idea of cooking had been limited to opening take-out containers. But when she'd mentioned it to Dr. Westbury, her mentor had been intrigued, and eager to start a clinical trial.

"Yes?" she asked as Josh closed the oven, before setting the timer and reclaiming the cookbook.

Josh offered a wicked smile straight out of his brother Chad's repertoire as he glanced from his handwriting to the recipe. "Can I make extra whip cream and save some for later? I also wrote a line or two about Megan swinging by after her second job. According to my trusty notebook, she wants to lift my spirits a bit, and a nice serving of whip cream would sure help."

"Sure," Kat said with a laugh. "Go ahead and double it."

Out the window, she saw Brody leaving the barn, carrying a toolbox. He gave her a wave and then headed for his truck. After yesterday in the wine cellar, she wanted more of him. But "serious" and "girlfriend" were labels that didn't fit with her life. Fling and Casual Sex? Those words worked for her. And she had an idea about how to win Brody over to her way of thinking.

"Josh, why don't you triple the recipe?"

BRODY PULLED UP to the house with a solid plan for the evening. First, a shower to wash away the grease from working on one of Moore Timber's trucks, then he'd find Kat and ask her to join him for a pizza in town. In a crowded restaurant—and A Slice of Independence was always packed, even on a Sunday—they could talk about Josh's treatment and keep their clothes on.

Of course, Kat had proven last night that a roomful of people wouldn't stop her from rocking his world in a wine cellar. But he could keep her out of the pizza place storage room while they split a pie.

He reached the sagging wraparound front porch, which he planned to rebuild now that the winter weather was behind them and they had money in the bank from selling the trucking company. As soon as he found the time. Between working with Moore Timber, volunteering with the search and rescue squad, and looking out for Josh, he needed more hours in the day. He had one foot on the steps when the door swung wide-open.

"Hey there, cowboy." Kat stood in the entryway to his family home wearing jeans and a button-down shirt that hugged her curves. Her long blond hair was pulled back into a ponytail. But the black ankle boots with the high, thin heel . . .

Brody paused on the porch steps. He had a plan for

tonight, but those shoes made him wish he could reconsider.

"I bet my mental image for tonight beats yours," she said, her green eyes blazing with mischief.

"Oh yeah?" He closed the space between them in two long strides, just in case his siblings were close by. Not that he was hiding his relationship with Kat. He'd seen the smirk on Chad's face when he slipped into the reception last night just moments after Kat returned. But his siblings didn't need details, and Brody didn't have a clue what would come out of her mouth next.

"I have two words for you." Her voice hit a sultry note that drove him damn near crazy. "Whip cream."

The best two words he'd heard all day.

"I was thinking pizza," he said. "And while you might win points for creativity, my idea gets us both fed while you tell me about your day."

"My day?" She raised an eyebrow. "I spent the last hour sitting at the table you made wondering if you'd ever thought about bending me over it and binding my ankles to the table legs."

His imagination followed her words, summoning the image. His body hardened, sending one message to his brain: *I want that.*

"Kat—"

"Once you had me there, I wonder where you'd put the whip cream."

Heat, need, desire roared through him. He stepped closer, pressing her back against the door. "I swear there is something about you that is so goddamn irresistible."

"My mouth?"

"That's part of it."

His hands found hers. Fingers interlaced, he drew her arms up, pinning them against the solid wood door. He didn't give a damn who saw, he had to touch her, taste her. His lips brushed hers, stealing a kiss.

"You taste like sugar and whiskey," he murmured.

"Bourbon," she corrected. "I've been baking pies with Josh."

"Are you done with my brother?"

She nodded. "Megan arrived for a visit. They took his creation and escaped into the barn."

"If Josh ran off with the pie, how are we going to eat the whip cream?"

"I have a few ideas."

"As much as I'd like to hear them all . . ." He released her hands, forcing himself to step back and stick to his plan. "I need a shower. And then I'm taking you out for pizza."

She arched an eyebrow. "You don't need to woo me with food when I've offered whip cream sex."

"I'm not wooing." He headed for the main stairs leading to the farmhouse's second story. "Tonight ends with pizza."

"If you say so." Her laughter followed him up the stairs.

He'd stand by those words. But he had a feeling she wouldn't make it easy. Stepping under the water, he closed his eyes and gave his imagination free rein.

Kat bent over the kitchen table . . . Or better still, here with him in the shower. Little Miss Perfect's back pressed against the tile wall, her legs wrapped around him while he drove into her.

He wrapped his hand around his dick. If he wanted release, he'd have it here. His fist moved up and down, drawing him closer and closer with each stroke.

The way her hands looked pinned overhead. Her mouth. Her voice. . .

Every word that escaped between those full lips excited him, from the naughty, teasing ones to the words that offered an insight into who she was past and present.

He pushed aside the image of her mouth and focused on how she'd looked in his bed. Picturing it here, under the steaming hot spray of water, was as close as he could get. Once he stepped out of this shower, he needed to focus on what was best for the people he cared about. The family who needed his time and focus. And he was pretty damn sure that taking Dr. Katherine Arnold, the doctor who lived on the other side of the country, to his bed was not on that list.

FORTY MINUTES LATER, after Brody had cleaned up, checked in with his little brother via text—he knew better than to interrupt "pie time" in the apartment over the barn—and confirmed that Megan would be staying off the clock awhile, he snagged the last parking space in the lot behind A Slice of Independence.

"This place is packed," Kat said. "We might want to think about taking our pie to go. My hotel is not far from here."

"Tables turn over quickly." He took her hand and led her toward the screen door separating the picnic tables from the indoor seating area. "We'll place our order at the counter. And while we wait for a table to open up, you can tell me about Josh's first session."

She nodded, transforming from I-want-whip-cream-sex Kat to Dr. Katherine Arnold. "Your brother managed a Bourbon Pecan Pie today."

He listened to the details, making mental notes of the little signs she thought spelled progress as they waited in line. When they reached the counter, he ordered the daily special, a pizza topped with local sausage.

"According to his medical history," Kat continued as they moved away from the counter, joining a cluster of locals waiting for to-go orders or an open table. "The staff at the rehab facility used memory games as part of his therapy."

"Yeah, he hated those," Brody said. "Said they just reminded him of what he couldn't do. And they seemed childish."

"The key is balancing the frustration with success."

"And having pie as a reward helps," Brody said. "Or at least that's your theory."

"It's a little more complicated than that. To be honest, your brother is in pretty good shape. A lot of the patients I see with brain injuries suffer from debilitating side effects."

"Does cooking help them all?"

"No. And that is only one element. Our trial is designed to show that individuals suffering from TBI—

traumatic brain injury—need help dealing with their emotions while they work to recover their memory."

He heard the passion in her voice, punctuating each sentence. "You know, you seem to care a helluva lot more than his previous doctors."

"Part of what makes me one of the best," she said with a warm smile.

Brody cocked his head, studying her. "Why neuroscience?"

"It's one of the more difficult areas of medicine."

"You like the challenge." And you hate to lose, he thought. He suspected she'd spent enough time on the losing end of things growing up.

"I like coming out on top. But I'm also interested in how the brain works. How people build memories attached to emotions." Her expression became serious. "After I leave, you might want to look for another therapist. Someone Josh can talk to, call day or night if he feels overwhelmed. I'm not joking about the link between depression and brain injuries."

"Kat Arnold?"

Brody glanced over his shoulder and spotted Delilah Travis. A slim woman with short black hair, he'd known the young nurse for years. He still owed Delilah a thankyou for taking care of Josh when his brother was in the hospital, though he suspected she'd prefer a more intimate sign of the Summers family's gratitude from Chad. Brody placed Delilah at the top of the list of single women in Independence Falls who mourned Chad's move from single playboy to off the market.

"You probably don't remember me," Delilah said to Kat. "I was Missy Jackson's best friend back when we were kids. You were a few years ahead of us in school, but I spent a lot of time at the Jacksons' house while you were living there."

Kat nodded, her lips forming a thin line. "I remember Missy. How is she?"

"Not as good as you. Two years at the community college isn't Harvard. She is living by the university now. Last time I spoke to her, she was thinking about getting a waitressing job when her youngest starts school next year. Missy's little boy is just the cutest. What about you? Are you thinking about moving back or just visiting?"

"I'm here for work," Kat said.

"Kat's is one of the leading neurologists in the country," Brody said. "She flew out to help Josh."

"Wow." Delilah's eyes widened. "Pretty amazing what going to Harvard can do for you, huh? I guess more people from here should apply to those fancy East Coast schools. Though it probably helps that you had such an interesting childhood."

"Yes, it probably did," Kat said.

The words sounded like verbal daggers. Brody could feel the tension rolling off Kat in waves, threatening to turn into a hurricane.

Oblivious, Delilah turned to him, placing her arm on his forearm. "Brody, you have to tell me all about the wedding."

"It was nice," he said. "The bride and groom seemed happy."

"I want details," Delilah insisted. "Tell me about the dress."

"You'll have to ask my sister. I can tell you Georgia was a beautiful bride, but not much more."

Stepping back, he pulled his arm away and stole a glance at Kat. Anger lingered in her green eyes. Delilah's words about Harvard and her childhood had breached her armor. But possession mingled with the hurt. If Delilah touched him again—and heck, the black-haired nurse had always been forward to a point that left him feeling uneasy—Kat might release the storm brewing in her expression and attack. Verbally or physically, he wasn't sure. As much as he liked the hint of *he's mine* driving her fury, he didn't want to find out.

Brody reached for Kat's elbow. Back in New York, she might not need anyone to jump in and save the day. But right now she needed a rescue.

Chapter 11

KAT REMEMBERED THE chipped pink paint on the walls of the room she'd shared with Missy Jackson for 457 days, even though she couldn't recall the woman with the pixie cut. But the way Delilah placed her hand on Brody didn't exactly inspire warm, friendly feelings. And Delilah's oh-so-eloquent words about Kat's "interesting childhood" and her time at Harvard didn't help either.

Was it so hard to accept that she had a sense of agency in her life? Kat wondered. Harvard had opened up doors and given her opportunities. But her hard work and determination delivered success. No one ever offered her top marks simply because she'd grown up alone, passed from house to house. In fact most of the time they'd expected less of her.

She felt Brody's hand on her elbow. A warning that she shouldn't attack a woman for touching him? For dredging up feelings she'd rather keep buried?

"You know, this place is packed," Brody said. "I'm thinking we should cancel our order and go somewhere else."

He offered a cursory smile to the woman with the pixie cut. "See you around, Delilah."

"Say hi to your brothers for me," Delilah said with a wink. "We miss seeing them out."

Kat allowed Brody to blaze a path to the counter, watching as he smiled at the frazzled woman distributing orders. "Trish, can we cancel our sausage pie?"

The waitress spared Brody a smile. "I'll see if they've made it yet. If they have—"

"I'll take it." a young mom with one toddler balanced on her hip and the other clinging to her legs said, her eyes wide with relief. "If it is ready, I want it. Doesn't matter what they ordered."

"Done." Brody turned to the mother. "Casey, this one is on me. You can thank your husband for picking up an extra shift last week when we were short a driver."

"Will do, Brody." The child in her arms screamed, diverting Casey's attention.

"You know everyone, don't you?" Kat said as they headed for the exit.

Brody shrugged. "Small town."

She followed him out of the restaurant and into the packed parking lot. "You know, we didn't have to rush out of there."

"I didn't want to run the risk you'd hurt Delilah."

She shook her head. "I shouldn't have let her get to me. But going to Harvard wasn't a joyride."

"No, I don't imagine it was," Brody murmured.

"Especially not the way I did it," she continued, the words spilling out. "Alone, with no one to call when I aced a test, or passed the boards, or . . ."

Kat closed her lips, biting them shut, knowing she'd already revealed too much. Sob stories about medical school weren't exactly a one-way ticket to whip-cream sex.

But Delilah's words had brought that time in her life back into focus. And when Kat thought about school, the loneliness surfaced. The other students had a place to go when they closed the dorms for the holidays. She'd managed by making arrangements to stay with friends. But she never forgot the fact that she was on her own. This town, the people here, Missy Jackson's family—one of the many who'd handed her back to the social worker as quickly as they could—everything about Independence Falls had set her up to navigate the world alone.

"Where are we going?" she said, mentally pushing the depressing thoughts away. She wasn't the orphaned student anymore. She had a life. Back in New York she had a career, colleagues, and friends waiting for her.

And tonight she had Brody Summers. She focused on his broad shoulders as he led the way through the maze of parked cars. She let her gaze linger on the way his jeans outlined the shape of his perfect butt.

"I'm still taking you to dinner," he said as they reached his pickup.

"I wouldn't object to eating closer to home and the whip cream." She didn't need the getting-to-know-you dinner-date routine. This man had already unearthed more of her, from the memories she kept under lock and key, to the way she bowed to his control when the clothes hit the floor, than anyone in her life, past or present. Right now she wanted to lose herself in fantasy and sex.

"You haven't forgotten about dessert, have you?" she asked.

Brody opened the passenger side door and turned to face her, his brown eyes roaming over her. "Kat, every time I look at you I think about new ways to try dessert. I want you. I can't stop picturing you in my bed. But—"

"Tell me what you see," she demanded. "I don't need promises. We don't need to talk about tomorrow. Not now. Tonight, I'd like a chance to build new memories of this town."

As she said the words, the truth unraveled. She'd taken Josh's case and returned to Independence Falls to show this town how far she'd risen, to prove that she no longer needed them to want her. But after walking into the hotel lobby, and then bumping into Missy Jackson's former best friend, maybe she also needed to prove to herself that her recollections of this town wouldn't cripple her. And the best way she could think of doing that was to retrain her brain and build new memories.

"Please, Brody," she added. "Describe the picture in your mind and let's see if it lines up with mine."

His brown eyes stared into hers, and she saw the moment desire crushed the reasons on his I-shouldn't-take-Kat-to-bed list.

Not just desire, she thought. This man cares about

people, from his family to the total strangers he rescues. If you ask, he'll set aside his reservations. He'll crush the god-awful memories. He'll make you feel wanted tonight. And maybe the night after that . . .

Her body warmed to the thought. A mental picture of Brody's naked body hovering over hers formed in her mind.

But what if he claimed more than her body?

No, she had to draw the line at fantasy sex. To invest in another person's life, to trust in them knowing feelings changed and shifted—she couldn't travel that road. In the back of her mind she would always be counting down the days until she hit 457, the maximum number of days the state allowed a minor to remain with one foster family. She'd always be waiting for the cycle to end. It was better if she kept an eye on the door. If she started hoping that it would stay closed, that this time she'd finally found a place for her heart to call home . . .

No. She already had a home. New York. And there was Brianna to consider. One day that little girl might open up and let Kat in. Not to mention her job—

"Close your eyes." He issued the command with an undertone of sensual promise, and she obeyed, blocking the runaway what-ifs. Because tonight just might take the route she desired—straight back to the bedroom.

She heard him open what she suspected was the glove box. Placing a hand on her waist, he turned her around.

"Keep them closed," he warned.

Fabric touched her face and she jumped at the unexpected. "You're blindfolding me?"

"Yes."

She felt his fingers working at the back of her head, tying a knot in what a quick peek told her was a bandanna. Then his hand took hers. He guided her into the front seat of his truck and secured her seat belt.

"Brody Summers, you're full of surprises," she said, fascinated by the way she heard every detail of his movements as he settled into the truck.

"At the hotel the other night, you told me swimming would help. Consider this my version of a dip in the pool," he said as the pickup shifted beneath her, making a right hand turn out of the lot. "Ready to hear my plan?"

"Take-out Chinese? I love lo mein after sex," she said as they accelerated. *Wait, were they merging onto the highway?* She touched the side of the bandanna, determined to steal a peek.

"Dinner will be a surprise." He drew her hand away from her face and placed it back in her lap. "But for dessert, I picture you in my bed."

"Might be messy," she murmured, her excitement unwinding, rushing to the parts of her body begging to know what happened next.

"Not the way I see it," he said. "Your arms stretched out overhead, your wrists tied. Whip cream between your breasts waiting to be licked clean."

"That's one way to enjoy dessert." She shifted, her thighs rubbing together. The combination of the blindfold and his words left her flat-out aching for him.

"It might be better if I turn you over, tie your legs to the bedpost," he said. "I can picture you lying there while my fingers leave a trail of cream up the back of your calves, a touch in the curve of your knee, a dash on the back of your thighs. I'd start at the bottom and lick you clean."

"My hands?" The words escaped on an exhale, her chest rising and falling as her breathing detoured from calm and collected to erratic and wanting.

"Free to press into the mattress, lift your ass in the air and ask for more."

And oh God help her, his voice was a low growl.

She felt the truck merge right, slowing down then pulling to an abrupt stop. "Where are we?"

"Salem," he said.

"What?" How on earth had they ended up in the state capital when all the signs indicated a joyride leading straight to bed and bondage?

"You can take the blindfold off," he added, a hint of humor replacing his rough, needy tone.

Kat ripped off the bandanna. She blinked her eyes, adjusting to the soft light of dusk. Cars lined the city street. Salem was a world away from Manhattan when it came to metropolitan areas, but it wasn't Independence Falls. She couldn't demand an orgasm in the front seat of his pickup and expect no one would notice.

"Turn the truck around," she ordered.

Smiling, he took her hand, pulling the bandanna free from her grip. With every touch, her breasts begged to be next, followed by all the parts of her body he planned to cover in whip cream.

"Before we get to dessert, I'm buying you dinner.

There is a bistro here called A Taste of Paris that I think you'll like." Cupping her cheek with one hand, he leaned over and stole a brief kiss. "I'm going to feed you before I tie you to the bedposts."

"OK," she murmured. The sexual need lingered, outpacing hunger. But his tone didn't leave room for argument. One hand on the car door, she glanced back at him. "Independence Falls, the people there, they don't have a clue about your wild, dirty mouth, do they?"

"No." His deep brown eyes stared into hers. "Only you, Kat. I'm only wild with you."

Chapter 12

BRODY SCANNED THE menu, but it might as well have been written in French. The only thing he wanted was sitting beside him, using every excuse to touch him. A hand on his arm. Her thigh brushing up against his as she accidentally slid too far into the booth.

"Do I need to tie you up for dinner?" he murmured.

"Are you planning to feed me? One french fry at a time?" she teased, leaning close, her shoulder touching his.

"I might." He looked at her over the top of his menu. Her eyes sparkled as her hand moved to his thigh. Brody sucked a deep breath. Here, in the corner booth of the upscale restaurant, she looked like Kat, the supposed ER doctor he'd met in the airport hotel—daring, welcoming, and intriguing as hell. He realized that she was at home in a room peopled with strangers.

Or she was still turned on from the ride over.

His jaw tightened and he set the menu aside. Blind-folding a woman in the parking lot behind the pizza place, and opening the door to the way he wanted her, what the heck was he thinking?

It was the look in her eyes when Delilah talked about Harvard as if the fancy school had handed Kat the keys to the kingdom. But he could connect the dots. The little girl who'd tried to find a family at the Falls Hotel hold-ing her science project as proof she deserved a home, that kid didn't show up at an Ivy League school and wait for handouts. She'd fought her way to the top alone. She'd struggled, adapted, and changed.

And he was goddamn crazy about the woman she'd become. He'd blindfolded her and stolen her away from his hometown to remind her who she was now—a beau-tiful, sexy, smart woman who didn't need anyone feeling sorry for her.

"Do you feel at home in New York?" he asked after the waiter left with their order.

"Depends on how you define home."

Kat took a sip of her white wine, drawing his attention to her full lips. On the drive over, he'd stolen glances at her mouth. He'd been tempted to pull over and kiss her. Her lips were like a beacon, calling to his from below the blindfold.

"I feel alive there. And I love the diversity. People from all over the world meeting in one place. They all have different stories, but the focus always seems to be on the now," she said.

"Your friends in New York look at you and see a doctor

and the rest falls away." Logically, he understood, but the thought of cutting ties with the past felt foreign to him.

"Yes." She smiled. "Have you ever been? To the city?"

He raised an eyebrow. "There's more than one city."

"Not when you live in New York." Her calf brushed his under the table. It was too damn bad she'd traded in her short skirt for a pair of blue jeans.

"No, I've never been to the East Coast. My mother caught the travel bug when we were kids. Claimed she couldn't stay in one place."

"She just walked out? On all of you? I knew you lived with your dad in high school, but I didn't know your mom abandoned you."

"Yeah, she just up and left one day. After my dad got out of the army. When my sister was still little."

"There wasn't anyone else? A reason?"

"It wasn't my place to ask. My dad was a mess and he needed help. I pitched in with the laundry, made sure everyone got to school, and my dad, well, he took over the trucking company, working alongside my grandfather."

"Did you ever try to find her?" Kat asked, her wineglass poised at her lips.

"No." One word offered without a hint of regret.

"I can't imagine having family out there and not reaching out to them."

He knew his mother's abrupt departure from their lives left a lingering wound, more so for his siblings. But for him it was over and done. His job was to make damn sure Chad, Katie, and Josh never felt the pain of someone they loved giving up on them and letting them down again.

"Your father's out there," he pointed out, his defenses rising.

"My dad is in prison. And he's never been a part of my life."

"Same goes for my mom," he said. "Not the prison part, though I guess it is possible. But she is not in my life now."

Kat set her glass down, turned and stared at him, her head cocked to one side. "I've been wondering why you've stayed single. But I don't think you have lingering commitment issues."

"Is that your professional opinion, Doctor?" He shifted away, her words unsettling him. The way he saw it, he had major "commitment issues"—his family, work, search and rescue, the farmhouse he planned to fix up now that they had the money. The list went on and on, pulling him in a dozen different directions.

"Yes," she said, sipping her wine. The waiter delivered their dinner, a burger for him, fish cooked in some sort of fancy bag for her, and an order of rosemary fries.

"You're wrong," he said as the server rushed away. "I have a pile of commitment issues. Right now, Josh tops the list. But it has always been one of my siblings or the company, needing my time and attention. When I settle down and get married, I want to do it right. I want to spend the rest of my life giving my wife everything I have in me to give. And everything she needs."

"That's a lot to offer," she said, steam rising up from her fancy plate of fish.

Only to someone who'd spent years believing she'd never make the cut, he thought. Her hand tightened around the stem of her wineglass, and for a second he thought it might snap. Raw emotion swam in her green eyes. Awe mixed with confusion, as if the two feelings had been tossed in a blender. But she quickly masked it.

"What would you ask for in return?" Kat set the glass down and claimed her fork. Stabbing the fish, she pulled it apart.

"I'd like to have a family one day. But to be honest, I'd settle for waking up next to the woman I love every morning and knowing she has the same deep feelings for me that I have for her."

Kat drew in a deep breath, her eyes wide as her fork remained buried in her food. Judging from the look of wonder he saw on her face, she'd never considered that anyone might feel that way about her. Seeing that look, Brody felt his temper rising at the injustice delivered to the woman sitting beside him. If only he could he'd erase the pain of her past. It fucking killed him that this woman had never known love, the kind that bound a family together.

He set his burger down on his plate before the anger pulsing through him flattened his meal. If he could turn back the clock, he'd find Kat hiding in the corners of his high school and he'd do something to make her believe she deserved love. Hell, he might take a swing or two at all the foster parents who'd sent her packing.

"You're like the dream contestant for one of those re-ality shows," she said. "Just think, you could have your own TV show with a hot tub full of women waiting for the chance to fall in love with you."

After witnessing her unmasked emotional response to his words, seeing the awe tinged with confusion, he let her hide behind humor. "Yeah, but then I'd have to tell millions of viewers, including my friends and family waiting back home, that I want whip-cream sex. At least once a month."

"Kinky sex is a deal breaker, huh?"

He picked up a rosemary fry without taking his eyes off her. "Seems that way."

"You can't find a woman in Independence Falls who wants you to tie her up and lick you clean?" she asked, her leg "accidentally" brushing his again.

"To be honest, I haven't been looking all that hard," he said. But who gave a damn about the past, when he'd found her now?

She set her fork down and rested her hand on his forearm, her fingers pressed into the sleeve of his flannel shirt. "It's because you're so sober. They assume you want serious sex."

He laughed, allowing his temper over her rotten childhood to fade. He wanted to keep her here, laughing and joking with him. "Serious sex? Sounds pretty damn boring."

"Like two people who keep their clothes on instead of using them for bondage," she murmured, reclaiming her fork.

"Kat." He set his burger down again. He was hungry, but he didn't want the fancy French version of an American classic. Lowering his arm, he placed his hand on her thigh, his fingers running up it. "There is nothing serious about what I'm picturing right now."

SHE SURVIVED DINNER. Barely. Every stolen touch, every movement of his body, propelled her desire forward. They'd reached the car and she was tempted to beg him to pull over. She'd wanted him to *take her* in the front seat of his truck. And if her mind was ready and willing to grant him control—here, now, *anywhere*—she knew for a fact the physical pull bordered on overwhelming.

Let it sweep her up and drag her under like a fast moving current, she thought. Focusing on the bulge in his jeans kept her mind from playing back his words.

I want to spend the rest of my life giving my wife everything I have in me to give. And everything she needs.

She'd spent years fantasizing about his warm smile and beautiful eyes, but she'd never stopped to fully picture the boy as a grown man. His broad shoulders tapering off to his waist, not an inch of fat on him. That she'd found anyway. She would be happy to resume her search. The muscles that screamed: *I can tie you up, hold you down and make you scream with pleasure.*

And she'd certainly never fantasized about the grown-up Brody's desire to settle down and give the woman he loved everything. She never focused on the future with anyone—real or fantasy. If she began dreaming about forever, the inevitable moment would come when the rug was ripped out from under her. The person holding her heart would show her the door, wishing her the best, and then go on with his life as if she'd only been a momentary blip.

"Kat?"

She turned her attention back to him as he sped down the driveway to his home. "Yes?"

Stopping, he threw the truck into park and glanced at her, his gaze burning with reckless, unrestrained need. Kat drew a deep, unsteady breath. The physical she understood. Momentary desire, no matter how potent, was as fleeting as an orgasm.

"Where's the whip cream?" he asked, his low tone teasing her senses.

"In the fridge. I'll race you."

She hopped down from the truck and ran for the screen door leading to the kitchen. Footsteps sounded behind her. And Brody's strong arms banded around her, drawing her back against his chest. Her hands wrapped around his forearms, pressing into the bulge of muscle. So much strength . . . She arched into his hold and felt the hard proof that he wanted her.

"I want you to go inside and head upstairs. My door is the first on the right when you reach the landing." He lowered his mouth to her neck, brushing a gentle kiss. "I want you in my bed."

"How?" Her hips rocked against his erection. "Tell me what you see."

He loosened his hold, his hands capturing her hips.

Holding her tight against him, he murmured, "Take off your clothes, lie on my bed and close your eyes. Wait for me. Let the excitement build. By the time I walk into the room, I want you wild."

His hands fell away, but he didn't step back. Hovering close, Brody Summers offered a wall of muscle. He didn't push her to go, or leave her standing alone in the dark corner of the yard, waiting for her to race into the house. He gave, she realized, as much as he took. Maybe more. Even when it came to games firmly based in desire and mutual need.

Focus on his bed, the whip cream, and this moment . . . nothing more.

"Bottom shelf on the right." She moved to the house. "The whip cream."

Opening the door, she slipped into the kitchen and headed for the stairs. Inside his bedroom, she surveyed the space. The furniture stole her breath away. Everything from the cherry dresser to the rich red textured wood posts of his bed frame defined this place as his.

She walked over to the room's focal point and ran her hand over the large wooden footer. The bed dominated the room. The square posts rising up from the four corners gave the piece a distinctly masculine feel due to the blunt, sharp lines.

Standing in the center of Brody's space, she stripped off her shirt, tossing it over an easy chair. It was possibly the only piece of furniture that wasn't made from the trees lining this property. Her pants and underwear followed, until she stood naked in his room, surrounded by the handcrafted testaments to his love of this land.

Climbing onto his bed, she drew comfort from the fact that Brody Summers was tied to Oregon. The job he loved involved saving people on the mountains cloaked in darkness beyond the walls of a home that had been in the family for generations. His room was filled with pieces of this place, carefully molded to highlight the best of Oregon.

Lying back on his bed, she closed her eyes. She could appreciate the natural beauty. But when she thought of what Oregon had to offer, her list stopped at Brody Summers.

The door opened and she heard his footsteps on the floorboards. Desire pulsed through her with each sound. His hand touched her ankle and she let out a gasp.

"Roll over, Kat."

She obeyed, spreading her legs wide as her feet pushed against the footboard's smooth surface. Planting her palms on the bedspread, she rose to all fours and rocked back and forth, creating the fantasy he'd described in the truck.

"Like this?" She glanced over her shoulder.

"Yes."

Her gaze fell to his hands holding the whip cream. She raised an eyebrow. "No ropes?"

His brown eyes darkened, narrowing in on her legs. "I couldn't wait. I had to taste you." Setting the container on the bed beside her leg, his gaze met hers. "May I?"

She nodded, holding back the words *Take me, make me yours!*

"Close your eyes, Kat."

She obeyed. Lowering her head, she allowed her hair to fall forward as she blocked out everything beyond the here and now. She heard the rustle of clothes and the pop of the Tupperware container opening. The bed shifted, forcing her to adjust as he climbed up beside her.

"Oh," she gasped. The cool feel of whip cream on the back of her calf surprised her senses.

His fingers swirled higher, running up to her knee. His touch disappeared and returned with another dollop of sugary goodness on the back of her thigh.

"Your mouth, Brody." She allowed her knees to slide farther apart on the bedding. "I want your mouth."

"Not yet." His fingers traced small circles, moving upward over her backside.

"Brody," she growled, rocking back and forth, perilously close to begging for his fingers to slide inside her, followed by his tongue and his cock.

"When I first saw you," he said, his voice low and rough, suggesting his need matched hers. "I thought you looked pretty damn perfect."

"And now?"

Whip-cream-covered fingers touched her low back and moved down, down, down . . . She opened her eyes, glancing over her shoulder. On his knees behind her, his hands on her butt, he looked like a wicked version of her fantasies. This wasn't the boy who fixed her shoes. This was the man who gave her the best damn orgasms of her life.

"What do I look like now?" she demanded, her voice low and needy.

"Messy."

Lowering his mouth to her back, Brody ran his tongue through the cream. Everything slipped away, her world narrowing to the feel of his lips on her skin, licking her clean.

"I warned you," she gasped.

"Hmm." His mouth remained focused on her.

Just when she thought he'd finished teasing her and was ready to reach for a condom—*please God let him have a condom*—his lips retraced the path up her legs, moving between them. The pleasure rose up, rushing forward—

"Not yet, Kat," he murmured. "Not yet."

"Wait, what are you doing?" she protested, her eyes wide, her body burning for the promised orgasm. "You can't stop now."

"Roll over Kat."

Lying on her back, she watched him move to the hand-carved nightstand, open a drawer and retrieve a condom. Within seconds he was on the bed with her, his body hovering over hers. He kissed her, long and slow, as one hand moved between her legs.

"I'm ready," she murmured, breaking the kiss. "Please, Brody."

His gaze locked with hers. "You say that word and I'm lost, Kat. Please. That's all it takes and I'm lost in you."

"Please," she whispered, rocking her hips up to meet his.

Brody listened, gently pressing into her. There it

was—a flash of pure possession in his brown eyes. This man didn't need ropes to dominate her. She was ready and willing to melt into him, to give him everything in silent response to the wanting written on his face.

"Please, Brody. More." The words escaped on a gasp of pleasure. He increased the pace, thrusting harder, faster, deeper.

"I want you, Kat." Holding his weight on his elbows, Brody hovered over her. "You're mine."

No. She didn't belong to him, not beyond this moment.

"You're mine," he repeated, his voice a low rasp as he thrust into her, driving her toward physical release.

She focused on the sexual challenge in his words, narrowing her world to the feel of his powerful body. "Then take me."

He let out a low growl as he pushed her closer and closer . . .

"Brody!" She tumbled over. "Oh Brody."

Pleasure washed over her, taking her to a place of momentary bliss. He might desire her now, but she'd wanted him for so long. And now, in this moment, he was hers.

But like the orgasm, it wouldn't last. She couldn't open herself up to the possibility. If she did, the hurt, the rejection, would crush her. And it would come. It always did.

Still, she'd hold tight to this moment. And maybe demand another before she headed home to New York.

Chapter 13

WAKING UP IN Brody's bed offered a different view of Independence Falls. Dawn peeked over the mountains beyond his window. But the postcardworthy scenery was nothing compared to the man in the room. The six-foot-plus wall of muscle who'd proved last night that he knew how to use every inch of his perfect body to his advantage—and hers—stood by the dresser pulling a shirt over his head.

"Going somewhere?" she asked, rising up on her elbows.

"Work." His gaze lingered on her chest.

"Maybe you could call in sick?" She sat up, allowing the sheet to drift to her waist. "With a case of the Monday morning blues."

"I'm not heading to the Moore Timber offices. Though with Eric away on his honeymoon, I need to swing by at some point." He pulled on his jeans, opened a drawer and withdrew a pair of socks. "The sheriff called. A teenager went for a hike in the Valley of the Giants on Saturday and never came back. He didn't call the BLM—the Bureau of Land Management—before he went in, just told some friends. No one is sure how he got in there. The old logging roads leading up there are a mess this time of year.

"His family reported him missing early this morning. The police think the kid might have run away and decided to set up an illegal camp on protected land, surrounded by five-hundred-year-old trees."

"Maybe he has his reasons." She drew the sheet up, covering her bare chest. She'd had a laundry list of whys when the police threatened to arrest her for spending the night hidden by those trees. Seventeen years old and facing move number twelve, she'd run before the social worker showed up. The cops had let it slide that time. And the next day she'd received her entrance letter to Harvard. She'd turned her life around. But it hadn't been easy. And for some it was downright impossible.

"For building a fire in an old growth forest?" Brody secured a long, sheathed knife to his belt. "Even this time of year, the kid could start a forest fire. And who knows if he packed in enough food and water?"

"He probably didn't, not if he was running away." She hadn't. She'd just fled, driven by overwhelming teenage emotions and logic that forgot things like food and water. "I hope you find him."

"Me too." He dropped a kiss on her forehead. "I should be back tonight. And when I return, we should talk."

"I'm in as long as the 'conversation' involves dessert."

"Kat, I'm serious—"

"So am I." She reached up, wrapping her arms around his neck, holding his lips close to hers. "I'm yours." *For a few more nights.* "Go out there and save the kid. Then come home and take me."

BRODY FOLLOWED THE retired Bureau of Land Management forester through the trees. Hiking across the lush, fifty-odd-acre parcel lined with five-hundred-year-old trees offered a window into what Oregon's forests looked like hundreds of years ago. It was a great way to start the day, apart from the fact he was here on a mission. And he'd left a beautiful, naked woman in his bed.

"I doubt anyone's here," Mitch said, moving down the narrow path. The search and rescue team had voted to split up, each taking one of the more experienced guides with them. "No trucks by the trail head," Mitch continued. "And getting up here on those logging roads isn't easy."

"My truck did all right." Brody easily kept pace with the sixty-year-old volunteer. "One of Eric Moore's crew harvesting the private parcel north of here reported smoke."

Mitch frowned. "Campfires aren't allowed up here. Although hell, neither is camping. But it happens from time to time."

"Tourists?"

"No, they follow the rules and contact the BLM to

find out if the roads are open before planning a trip. They stick to the trail, get their pictures with the giants, and head out. Teenagers are always the troublemakers."

"How often do you find runaways up here?" Brody asked, scanning the forest beyond the path.

"Every couple of years. Like I said, it is hard to get here. Most of the time we catch them before dark and send them packing. Your friend, the visiting doctor, she was the last one to camp more than a night or two."

"Kat?" Brody's eyebrows shot up. She hadn't said a word when he'd left, except . . .

Maybe he has his reasons.

And Brody had a feeling he understood hers too.

"Kat Arnold. She was a handful. But I guess any kid kicked to the curb and left with nothing ends up taking a wrong turn or two. I remember when the cops came they cut her a break. The officer in charge said she was due to move again. Claimed nobody wanted her. The previous foster family just wanted the check for housing her."

I want her. The word roared in his mind.

"And to think she went on to become a city doctor," Mitch continued, shaking his head. "I bet some of those families are kicking themselves right about now. If they'd adopted her, she would probably be sending money back to them."

Brody picked up the pace. The thought of a teenage Kat sitting up here to avoid the people who wanted the money she represented, not the child herself, tore at him. He hated the thought of anyone using her. Smart, determined Kat deserved love, dammit, back then and now.

The path turned muddy and he slowed his steps. Where did that leave him? Down on one knee promising forever? Trying to juggle a long distance relationship with Josh's recovery, his jobs—paid and volunteer—and the work on the house? Falling in love with her?

"Smell that?" Mitch said.

Brody pushed his own questions aside and focused on the scent of burning timber. "Yeah, someone built a fire around here recently."

The experienced forester headed down the path without a word, stopping abruptly twenty feet ahead. He pointed to boot marks on the ground. "Not much to take pictures of over there. The famous trees are behind us."

Brody nodded and followed the trail. Behind a pair of giant firs, he spotted a navy blue sleep bag. A makeshift fire pit filled with ash stood a few feet in front of the kid. Anger took hold and Brody ground his teeth. Those flames could have destroyed a piece of protected forest, burning trees that had stood on this ground for hundreds of years. And after it erased the Giants, the flames would move on, threatening homes and possibly lives.

It was hard to imagine this kid had a solid reason for taking the risk and building that campfire.

"Hey there," Brody said, kneeling beside the sleeping bag. "Are you Jason Matts?"

"Ah fuck." The teen rolled over and opened his eyes.

"Your parents reported you missing. They're worried about you, Jason," Brody said in the same no nonsense voice he'd used to keep his siblings in line when they were younger. "And one of the logging crews spotted the smoke from your fire," he continued. "You know camping and building fires is not allowed here, right?"

"Yeah, I know." Jason wiggled out of the sleeping bag. Tall and skinny, the teen was like a beanpole. "I'm sorry about the fire. And setting up camp," the kid said as he rolled up his sleeping bag. "But I had to do something to get their attention. My parents are planning to move to Florida. My grandma is there. My uncle and cousins too. My dad wants us to live closer."

"You don't want to go, so you ran away," Brody said as Mitch checked the makeshift fire pit to make sure it was extinguished.

"Yeah." The kid pulled on his pack. "Can you imagine leaving all of this for fucking Florida? It's flat there. No mountains. No trees. Just a bunch of old people."

"And your family," Brody said. "Trust me, kid, you want to be where your family is. At the end of the day, they're what matters. And right now they're worried sick about you. So let's get you home."

But his thoughts drifted back to Kat as he led the kid to the parking area. His own family was here. He couldn't pack up and walk away from them because he took one look at Kat and thought, She's mine.

This community, the people here, his brother and sisters, and yeah even the falling down home that had been in his family for generations—they were all his too.

DUSK SETTLED OVER the mountains as Brody pulled up to the farmhouse. After returning Jason to his parents, who'd threatened to ground him for the next year—in Florida—for running away, Brody had swung by the Moore Timber office and focused on trucking schedules. His sister, who ran Moore Timber's biomass initiative, wanted another semi to haul away the by-products of the timber harvest, the branches and other pieces that generally fell to the forest floor. Brody had found a used truck for sale, but the mechanical inspection raised a few red flags.

Holding the paperwork on his arm, he walked into his kitchen. Kat sat at the head of the table, surrounded by his brothers. Beer bottles and an empty pizza box lined the table.

"Brody," Chad called, raising his beer. "Just in time."

"You saved me a slice?" He went to the fridge and withdrew a cold microbrew before claiming the vacant seat opposite Kat.

Smiling, her green eyes dancing with amusement, Kat laughed. "You're in time for another embarrassing story. Your brothers are telling me all of your dirty secrets."

"We felt she deserved to know," Chad said. "Rumor has it she woke up here this morning."

"They caught me rifling through the cabinets for the coffee," Kat said.

"And I wanted to prove that there is nothing wrong with my long-term memory," Josh added, pushing the pizza box in Brody's direction.

"Kat, did you ever visit the coast when you were growing up?" Chad asked.

She nodded. "I went on a class trip to the aquarium."

"We should take you back sometime," Chad said. "They've made a lot of improvements."

"I'd love to see it again," she said, lifting her beer to her lips. "But I'm curious about what it has to do with an embarrassing Brody story."

"Cut right to the good stuff," Josh said, rubbing his hand. "I like that about you."

Yeah, me too, Brody thought, reaching for a slice.

Kat let out a bark of laughter and his hand stilled. Did she realize how at home she looked with his family? Seeing her smile, watching her with his brothers, the tension from his day slipped away.

"Not the aquarium, but the coast," Chad explained. "A bunch of the football players took a trip to the coast to grab some of the Clam Shack's famous chowder."

Chad reached for his beer and Josh took over telling the story. "Some of the cheerleaders went along and dared the guys to take a dip in the ocean. Brody accepted the challenge."

"But as he dove in," Josh jumped in, "a wave rose up and ripped his shorts off him."

Kat turned to him. "You went swimming in the Pacific without a wetsuit in, what, September?"

"November," Chad corrected. "And he was in his boxers."

Kat raised an eyebrow but didn't say a word about the hotel pool.

"The wave ripped them right off and took them out to sea," Josh added. "Brody had to walk out in front of everyone without a stitch on him. And the way I heard the tale, the cold didn't exactly do him any favors."

"Hey," Brody protested.

"You might want to keep him out of cold water," Chad added.

Kat laughed. "I'm not worried."

"What about you, Doc?" Josh asked. "What is your most embarrassing story from growing up?"

Brody froze, the lukewarm slice in front of his lips. His brothers could joke about his high school mishaps all they wanted, but Kat didn't need to relive the worst moments of growing up here. And he could only imagine her long list of uncomfortable stories. He'd witnessed the old hurts coming back to haunt her, and he freaking hated that look in her eyes.

But her face lit up as she lowered her beer. "Oh I have a good one. And it involves your brother."

Chad raised an eyebrow. "Didn't realize you knew each other back then."

Brody's brow furrowed. As far as he knew, their one and only interaction had occurred in the art room. But there was nothing embarrassing about fixing a pair of shoes out of sheer necessity. "Kat—"

"Everyone knew Brody Summers," she said, taking another sip of beer and ignoring the note of warning in his voice. "And I was one of the many girls at Independence High who had a crush on your brother," she added.

"What?" Brody lowered the pizza.

"A crush?" Chad flashed a charming smile as he rubbed his hands together. "This should be a good one."

"Kat, how many beers have you had?" Brody demanded, scanning the empty beer bottles on the table.

"She's on her second, bro. We didn't get her drunk," Chad said. "Calm down and let her tell the story."

"My sophomore year, some of the guys from Brody's class threw a party in the woods," Kat said, accepting his brother's invitation. "They got their hands on a keg, built a bonfire and invited half the school. After my first beer, I decided it would be a great idea to declare my undying love for your brother."

Brody choked on his pizza and coughed. "What?"

Her undying love? He searched his memory trying to determine if the party he didn't remember—because hell, they'd taken a keg into the woods more than once—was before or after he glued her sneakers together.

"But I never got the chance." Kat pointed her beer at him before turning her attention to her audience. "I spotted him in the woods, removed from the party, and thought here is my shot."

"Don't tell me you caught him with his pants down," Chad said.

"No, I didn't." Kat shook her head. "Though I'm sure the girl with him would have preferred that. Instead your big brother was telling her—and I can't remember her name, even though I was insanely jealous of her at the time—"

"Lisa," Chad supplied. "Brody dated her for a while in high school junior year. Nice girl. With nice—"

"Chad," he snapped before his brother could comment on Lisa's breasts. Yeah, he remembered the girl and why he'd asked her out in the first place.

"Your brother was telling *Lisa*," Kat continued, "that he respected her too much to kiss her when she'd been drinking."

"Now how is that embarrassing for you, Doc?" Josh said.

"I was stuck in the woods, listening to a boy I had a crush on lecture a drunk girl—who looked like she wanted to abandon her clothes and jump him—about the right time for kissing, when Abby Greenwald, the most popular girl in my class, found me."

"Hey, I know Abby," Josh said. "She works at the animal shelter near the university."

"Of course she'd end up surrounded by puppies." Kat shook her head. "Abby Greenwald teased me for the rest of the year, telling everyone I'd been spying on Brody and Lisa."

"While Brody *talked* to the girl," Chad said. "Man, it is a miracle you ever got out of your own way for long enough to get laid in high school."

Brody growled, biting back the words, *I did just fine in high school*. Because what he'd done back then, who he dated, it didn't matter now that he took one look at Kat, smiling and joking with his family. He wanted to make her *his*. Upstairs, alone, away from these idiots he loved with everything he had.

Josh pulled out his notebook and pen. "I'm writing that one down. So I can tease you later, Doc. Next time you try to make me do one of those stupid memory card games, I'm going to remind you of your 'huge Brody Summers crush.'"

Kat laughed. "You'll still have to do the memory exercises."

"So I guess you're trying to tell us you spent last night talking with my brother?" Chad said.

"Enough," Brody said, pushing back from the table. He set his half-empty bottle of local brew on the table and reached for Kat's hand, drawing her up. "I trust you guys can make sure the bottles land in recycling?"

Chad nodded. "We got it, bro."

"Where are you going?" Josh called, as Brody led Kat out of the kitchen.

"To talk to your doctor," Brody called.

He led her up the stairs and into his room. After the solid wood door closed behind them, he turned to Kat. He captured her hips in his hands, holding her in front of him. "So about this crush—"

"It was nothing," she said, her smile fading.

"Did it start before or after I helped fix your lucky shoes?" he asked softly.

Her wide-eyed gaze met his and she stepped back, trying to break away from him. But he went with her, until her back pressed against the wall.

"You remember?" she said.

He nodded. "As soon as you told me who you were, I put the pieces together."

"I can't believe you remember that day. Or me." She let out a low laugh. "I thought you were cute before, but that day . . . the way you smiled, your skills with the Super Glue . . . you became my high school fantasy."

He stared into her eyes, his body tightening with each word, driven by desire and something more. Moving closer, he placed one hand on either side of her head, his body inches from hers. "Just how wild were these fantasies?"

She shook her head. "It wasn't like that. Most of the time I'd see you in the hall and I just wanted you to smile at me."

He frowned. "I didn't ignore you, Kat."

"No, but you weren't a part of my life either," she murmured, her gaze focused on his chest. "And I wanted your attention, all that kindness, focused on me. Just for a little while."

Every muscle in his body froze. Back then he'd thought she needed new shoes. He'd been blind to the fact that friendship would have carried her a lot further.

"And a kiss," she added, lifting her gaze to meet his. "I would have liked a kiss too."

The vulnerability in her green eyes took him back to the Falls Hotel parking lot. He ran the back of his hand over her cheek and she closed her eyelids. She didn't let anyone in. She didn't let them see the helpless girl she'd been. But he'd caught a glimpse. And now he wanted to take care of her.

"Kat, look at me," he said, capturing her face between his hands. She obeyed, opening her eyes and staring into his. "I'm going to kiss you now."

His lips captured hers, soft at first before demanding

more. A low growl escaped as she opened up to him, her tongue brushing his. Her fingers dug into his shirt as if she wanted to keep him right here, kissing her.

Don't let go.

But she pulled back, breaking the kiss. "Do you know what I'm picturing now?" she murmured, her hands running down his chest, heading lower and lower. "Do you want to find out if it lines up with your mental picture for tonight?"

"It does, Kat. Trust me."

She let out a low laugh. "You might want to hear the details first. We made caramel sauce today."

He listened, her words turning him on as she described all the ways she planned to cover her body with caramel. Hell, every time she rocked her hips against his, she could feel the hard proof that he liked the idea of licking her clean. But it wasn't the just caramel sauce that left him aching to strip off her clothes and take her on the bed.

It was Kat.

He was falling for the woman behind the fantasy.

Chapter 14

ON WEDNESDAY MORNING Kat watched Josh move around the kitchen, gathering ingredients for a chili. She'd spent three nights in dessert heaven. Now it was time to leave the sugar haze behind and face reality. Her time in Independence Falls was limited—and so were her nights in Brody's bed.

"After yesterday's brownie disaster, I'm ready for some real food. What about you, Doc?"

And there it was, another clue she couldn't ignore.

"I love a good chili." Though she couldn't envision eating it off Brody's body.

But then yesterday's brownies hadn't worked either. Plus they'd come out of the oven hard as rocks, stumping both her and Josh. She'd never claimed she could bake, but she had a growing faith in Josh's ability to follow a recipe. Of course, the chocolate syrup she'd picked up to go with the brownie disaster had added a fun twist to her night—especially when Brody offered his well-defined abs as her plate.

Josh stirred the pot once, set the wooden spoon beside the stove. "It just needs to simmer for a while."

"Why don't you have a seat," Kat suggested. "While it cooks."

"Don't tell me you want to play another one of those card games." Josh slid into the chair beside her at the handmade kitchen table. His red curls fell across his forehead. "I feel like a freaking kindergartener matching shapes," he added.

"No more games." She set her pen down and interlaced her hands. "You don't need them, do you?"

"What?" His eyes widened.

"You remembered the brownies we made yesterday. And you knew who I was when I walked into the kitchen."

"How do you know I didn't look at my notes? You've been spending every night here. Do you even still have a room at the hotel?"

"I do." She didn't point out the fact that he'd recalled a detail about her living arrangements or that she'd kept it for her own sanity. Even though she'd spent the past few nights with Brody, she needed to know she had a place to go that was hers, even if it was only a temporary room.

"How do you know I didn't check my notebook before you came down? After I heard you screaming my brother's name and calling him a god in the shower this morning."

"That was yesterday morning," she pointed out, burying her embarrassment. She thanked the same higher power she'd linked with Brody's name that Josh's older brother was out on another rescue, his second this week. "You remember," she said, focusing on her patient.

"Maybe." Josh shifted in his seat, staring down at the table. "I guess your cooking therapy is working."

"It's possible. Though it hasn't been long. I would guess you were on the road to recovery when I showed up. There is a lot we don't know about the brain. Sometimes people who suffered accidents like yours only lose their short-term memory for a few months. Some a few days. And sometimes it just comes back. Especially in patients who underwent brain surgery." She reached out and covered his hand. "Your memory has been coming back for a while now, hasn't it?"

"Yeah. But it is confusing. I'm not always sure I can trust it."

She squeezed his hand. "That's normal. It may take a while. And it might not come back completely."

He glanced up at her, his eyes bright with panic. "Does this mean I'm done? With the trial?"

"I'll need to confer with Dr. Westbury. This hasn't happened with any of the other patients. We've seen progress, but after months of following an established therapy plan."

She left out the part that he'd barely qualified. Hearing that others were so much worse off than him wouldn't help. And it might make him feel guilty about his recovery. But she couldn't risk skewing the outcome of the trial. For reliable results, they needed some semblance of uniformity.

"I can help you establish a long-term plan," she continued. "The confusion and the fear might linger for a while. The medication will continue to help with the depression, but the rest is about building a life that works for you."

"I can't go back to driving trucks and hauling timber."

"Is that what you wanted?"

"After we sold the business, I was thinking about picking up more shifts with Eric Moore's crews. Though I don't think they want me out there operating heavy machinery or chainsaws."

"Probably not," she agreed. "Maybe you could take on a different role?"

"I'm not sure I want to. Before the accident, I thought about buying some land and starting a vineyard. I'd toyed with going back to school to study viniculture." He smiled. "Megan really likes the idea."

"When I get back, let's talk about how to make your plan a success." She withdrew her hand and picked up her pen.

"You're leaving?"

She nodded, scribbling a quick note in his chart. "I'm taking the red-eye back to New York tonight."

"Why?" She heard the panic in his voice. Like many of the patients she met with, she'd quickly become a crutch for him. She made a quick note to find a therapist for him to meet with on a regular basis. Managing his feeling as he navigated his recovery would become a priority now that he'd regained pieces of his short-term memory.

"I have some personal business to attend to in New

York." She smiled. "Your siblings know. And I will be back Friday morning. You're stuck with me for another week after that. But this was a previously scheduled appointment I couldn't cancel."

"Must be an important patient if you're flying back across the country."

"It's personal." She closed the file and pushed back from the table. "You might want to check on your chili while I pack up. Your sister agreed to drive me to the airport and she should be here soon."

Josh headed for the stove and paused, turning to her. "Thanks for taking a chance on me, Doc. I picked up bits and pieces from Chad and Brody. I know coming back here wasn't easy for you. But I feel like I've been lost in a maze for months now. It's nice to find a way out."

"You're welcome. And for the record, 'easy' and I aren't exactly on speaking terms. I like a challenge."

"One more thing, Doc." He kept his focus on the steaming pot. "Do you think we could keep this between us until I finish finding my way out? I'm not ready to tell my brothers and sister. Megan knows. But I can't help feeling like I'm going to jinx myself. And there are still moments when I can't recall what happened five minutes ago. I know you and Brody are—" He waved the wooden spoon through the air. "—a thing. But—"

"I won't say a word." He was her patient and his needs came first. "We can talk more about how and when you want to share the news with your family, but for now my lips are sealed."

BRODY WORE HIS sour mood like a cloak. When he'd joined the Willamette Valley search and rescue squad he'd envisioned saving lives, not arriving too late to do a damn thing.

He stepped inside the kitchen, expecting the sweet smell of pie. Heck, he'd settle for cookies or cupcakes. Something sugary and sweet followed by a long shower with the doctor who'd taken over his kitchen.

Not to mention his bed, his mind—and possibly his heart.

"Where's Josh?" he demanded.

His little sister looked up from a pile of magazines. "He is in the apartment over the barn with Megan. I think he's planning to move out there. For the privacy. It's probably a good idea. I stayed here on Monday while Liam was on a job site overnight, and I swear it sounded like you were rebuilding furniture in your room."

Ignoring his sister, he peered into the pot on the stove and frowned. "That's not a pie."

"Josh made chili today," Katie said. "I think he's moving on from dessert."

He didn't give a damn what Josh cooked. But Brody thought bringing chili to bed was a stretch. Sure, he could work with the leftover chocolate syrup. Or heck, he would settle for tasting her. Either way, he wanted to devour Kat, make her scream over and over, then slide inside and take her. He wanted to lose himself in her, erasing the memories from his god-awful day.

He ran a hand over his face. "Where is Kat?"

"I drove the doctor to Portland. She's flying back to

New York tonight, remember? It was part of her deal from the beginning. She mentioned it the first day. Some appointment she couldn't break."

"What?" He shook his head, feeling as if he'd entered the twilight zone.

"She's coming back on Friday," Katie said. "Though we might want to talk about the look on your face. The next time she heads east, I have a feeling she plans to stay there. On the ride to the airport, she suggested that Josh is making progress and said she doesn't think he'll need her help long-term. But you kind of look like you might."

"I just had a bad day." Brody went to the cupboard, took out a bowl, and filled it with chili. If sugar and shower sex weren't in the cards, he might as well eat.

"What happened?" Katie closed the magazine, her teasing tone replaced with concern.

"A mountain biker reported a motionless body by a campsite. A couple of us hiked out to check on the guy and found a body. We carried him down on a stretcher. One of the guys found an ID at the site. He was a veteran, fought in Iraq. Who knows how long he'd been living up there with next to nothing to eat?"

"That's awful, Brody."

"Yeah, it was." Brody took a bite of the chili. It was worse than the brownies. He associated chili with meat and spice. This had neither. "Good thing Josh is making progress. His cooking stinks."

"Dr. Arnold didn't get into specifics," Katie said. "But Josh will need to find a local therapist. And we have to maintain a stable environment for him. I'm not sure what that means for Megan."

"She isn't part of the long-term picture." Brody took another bite of the bland bean dish. "We can't justify the expense of keeping her on if we can trust Josh is safe here by himself."

"I'm not talking about her paid position," Katie said. "Have you seen the way he looks at her?"

Like he wants to get laid. Brody knew the feeling, and he'd be willing to bet he looked at Kat the same way. But shit, if he was being honest, he wanted a helluva lot more than kinky sex. He wanted a place in her life. The opportunity to take care of her long-term.

But now she'd flown back to New York to attend to God knows what, offering a striking reminder that her life was there and his was here.

"I think Josh is falling for Megan," his sister said, pulling him back to their conversation.

"I wouldn't count on Josh lining up to reserve the Willamette Views Vineyard for his special day anytime soon," Brody said. "Not in his condition."

"You might be right. But speaking of weddings." Katie held out her hand and wiggled her fingers. An enormous square rock sparkled under the kitchen lights.

"About damn time." Brody dropped his spoon and took her hand. "When did Liam propose? And how have you been sitting here this whole time without saying a word?"

"I was waiting for you to notice," she said.

"Sorry." Brody shook his head. He'd been so focused on Josh's doctor that he hadn't noticed the rock on his little sister's finger.

"Liam proposed last night under our trees," Katie said. "He wanted to wait until after Georgia's wedding."

He raised an eyebrow. "Your trees?"

"The place where—"

"You know what, I don't think I want to know."

She picked up the magazine. "I'm looking for a dress. We're thinking soon. Probably a weekend in Vegas. I want to save our money for the house and the stables. They're breaking ground next week, and once it's done, I'll be able to take in dozens of neglected or abused animals."

Josh was supposedly on the road to recovery—though Brody wanted to talk to Kat about what that meant. He needed details. Was his little brother regaining his memory or simply learning to follow a recipe?

He'd sit down with Kat when she got back. And they'd discuss a lot more than his little brother's memory. But right now he needed to focus on the fact his baby sister was getting married. And heck, Chad was close to asking Lena to spend the rest of her life with him.

Brody picked up his spoon and dug into the chili. If they all moved on, leaving the house they'd grown up in, where did that leave him?

Carrying a stranger's body down the mountain on a damn litter so that the veteran could receive the honor he deserved.

Pushing the depressing memory from today aside, Brody nodded to the magazine. "What are you thinking for the dress?"

"You want to talk bridal gowns?"

He nodded. It beat thinking about the questions pilling up in his mind about his little brother's doctor, or his long hike carrying a corpse.

Katie's face lit up as she launched into a detailed description of her ideal wedding gown. Half the words—bustle and chiffon—were meaningless to him. But he loved seeing her smile as if life had granted her everything she wanted.

Chapter 15

TWICE A MONTH Kat sat down with her past. The crowded elementary school cafeteria in Brooklyn looked nothing like the small-town lunchroom in Independence Falls, but the weary, yet hopeful expression on the fourth grader across the table was strikingly familiar.

"How's school?" Kat asked, setting aside her all-beef organic burger. After her first visit, seven months ago, she'd learned to bring her own lunch, and one for Brianna. The smell of the cafeteria food made her stomach turn. Eating it was far worse.

The little girl shrugged, picking at the well-seasoned french fries made from upstate New York potatoes. Kat waited, hoping for one of Brianna's rare one-word answers. OK, good, sucks—she'd take anything.

In the back of her mind Kat wondered if she was wasting her time. She'd flown across the country to have lunch with Brianna, and still the kid wouldn't talk to her.

"I spent the past few days on the West Coast. In Oregon," Kat said, filling the silence. Brianna's eyes widened as if she had revealed her recent trip to Mars. "It's nice out there."

Especially this one man. . .

But she couldn't tell the child who spent one hour twice a month sitting silently across the table from Kat about Brody. That would be crazy. Like taking two redeye flights to have lunch with a ten-year-old.

"After lunch, would you like to take a walk?" Kat suggested. The last time she spoke with Brianna's social worker Kat had begged for help. She wanted to make this work. This child had been placed in foster care after her mother died—just like her. Brianna's father wasn't in the picture and her older sister was placed in a different foster care home. Every time she sat down with the quiet, sullen child, Kat felt like she was looking in the mirror. She wanted to wrap her arms around the little girl and promise to make it better, to tell Brianna that she wasn't alone.

But first she had to get to know the girl. And the social worker had suggested Kat "express an interest in her school."

Brianna nodded, pushing the food away. "I'm ready."

Words. Kat's mouth fell open, but she quickly masked her surprise and scrambled to pack up the leftovers. In the hall, Brianna took a left and Kat followed, walking slowly at her side, noting the bright, cheerful art displays on the bulletin boards.

"I'm moving." Brianna kept her gaze on the polished floors.

"Oh?" The social worker hadn't mentioned anything.

"The family I'm with can't keep me anymore."

"Brianna." Kat froze and turned to the child. The way Brianna said those words, as if she were a pet who needed to be returned to the pound due to an allergic family member—it tore at her heart. Logically, Kat knew it was more complicated. But still—

"And I was thinking." The child looked up at her, hope swimming in her ten-year-old eyes. "I was thinking you might want to adopt me. Because you keep coming back."

Kat fought to hide her shock. But judging from the way the weariness returned to Brianna's face, she failed. She spent two hours a month with this little girl. They hadn't even graduated to weekend day trips. And still she qualified as the most steady presence in Brianna's life. Her stomach flipped and she regretted the few small bites of her burger.

The little girl drew a deep breath. "I'm smart, I stay out of trouble—"

"I'll talk to your social worker. Mrs. Henly." There were so many obstacles. Kat would need approvals. And with her job, the hours and travel . . . But she refused to stand here and listen to this child list her credentials.

"I can't make you any promises," Kat said. "But I will do my best."

The bell rang signaling the end of the lunch period. Children and teachers poured out of the cafeteria and classrooms.

"OK," Brianna said.

Kat nodded. "I should take you back to class."

Taking the child's hand, she navigated the busy hallway until they reached the door to the classroom. "Brianna?"

The child looked up her, her expression schooled into an impartial mask.

"For the record, I want to adopt you," Kat said, offering the words no one had given her as a child. "No matter what your social worker says, please don't forget that."

Eyes wide, Brianna nodded. "I won't."

FIVE MINUTES LATER Kat walked down the streets, excitement driving her hurried steps. For years she'd pushed the idea of finding a husband and starting a family aside. In theory, she wanted children. But whenever she thought about meeting a man, opening up to him, trusting he would want her tomorrow and the day after that . . . fear rose up and she slammed the door on the idea of family.

But she wanted to be a part of this little girl's life. She mentally flung open the doors to her spare bedroom, painting the walls a bright pink.

Kat froze in the middle of the sidewalk, ten feet from the subway entrance. What if Brianna hated pink? She didn't even know the child's favorite color.

She reached into her purse and withdrew her phone. She could learn. And if the state agreed, if she passed the test, she could transform her apartment into a home. She could make this work. There was plenty of room in her two-bedroom Manhattan apartment. She lived in a stellar school district, according to her neighbors with young children. And she could afford a nanny.

Pressing her cell to her ear, she called Brianna's social worker and left a message, making it clear she would do whatever it took to adopt the little girl.

After leaving the message, she headed for the subway, plans rushing through her head. She tried to set them aside until she heard from the social worker. Right now she needed to return to her patient—and his brother.

Brody.

Her smile faltered. But only for a second. She'd known from that first night in the hotel that her fling with Brody Summers would lead to a dead end. It was a fantasy. Nothing more.

Today she would return to Oregon and enjoy one more week with Brody Summers. Bondage, blindfolds, and whip cream—she wanted it all. Because when she came back to New York, her life would change forever.

THE NEXT MORNING, the cab company dropped Kat off in front of the Summers family farmhouse. Wearing the same skinny black jeans, long sleeve blouse, and ankle boots that she'd slept in on the plane, Kat headed for the front door. She needed a cup of coffee before she sat down with Josh and determined a plan for his future. One that hopefully included him telling his siblings about regaining his memory.

She knocked and heard Chad's voice calling for her to come in. Kat found the middle Summers brother in the kitchen with Lena.

"Hi, have you seen Brody?" she asked, heading for the coffeepot.

Chad hesitated.

"Did he get called out?" she probed, glancing at Lena. Even in her security uniform, her blond hair tied back in a bun, Chad's girlfriend looked like she belonged in a fashion spread with the golden retriever curled at her feet.

"He's headed to The Lost Kitten," Lena said.

Her brow furrowed. The name sounded vaguely familiar. "The what?"

"The strip club on the other side of the university," Chad said with a sigh. "About an hour from here."

She let out a laugh. Forty-eight hours had passed since she'd seen Brody and now he was at a strip club on a Friday morning? "Someone there called for search and rescue?"

"Josh. Though he didn't exactly call. The kid left a note," Chad said. "And Brody flipped out."

"Can you call Brody and ask him to turn around? I'd like to go with him." She raised the coffee mug and took a sip.

"I can drop you off on my way to work." Lena stood and Hero moved to her side. "I'm covering a shift for a coworker."

"And working straight through the night." Chad frowned. "You'll keep Hero with you?"

"Always," Lena said, dropping a kiss on his lips before heading to the screen door. Kat took one last sip of her coffee and followed her out.

Ten minutes into the drive Lena glanced over at her. "You're worried about him. Josh."

"He's making progress," Kat acknowledged, knowing she couldn't say more without breaking the promise she'd made to her patient. "But this isn't a good side. Sexual promiscuity is often associated with brain injuries. Is this the first time he's run off to a strip club? Did he go before?"

"I wouldn't know," she said. "I moved to Independence Falls not long before Josh's accident. But given the way Brody stormed out of the house, I doubt it."

"Brody's overprotective," Kat said.

"Of everyone he cares about. And I think you're on that list. I doubt he'll be happy to see you here."

"We're not dating." The words spilled out like a reflex.

"Do you care about him?" Lena asked, her gaze focused on the road. "If you don't, please do not lead him on. That man has given everything for his family, his work, this town. From what Chad's told me about his brother, Brody deserves to find someone who will give him everything in return."

Kat looked at the dog lying on the truck's front bench between them, happily chewing a toy. "I don't have much to offer him. My life is on the East Coast. He knows that. We've been clear. This is just a fling."

Lena shook her head. "That man looks at you as if you belong with him. Trust me, I know the look."

"It's not what you think," Kat insisted, folding her arms across her chest as she turned to the window.

He looks at me as if I belong in his bed, she thought. And she wanted to be there. For one more week.

A short while later they rounded the bend in a two-lane country road and The Lost Kitten appeared. The two-story structure looked like every other restaurant in the middle of nowhere Oregon apart from the neon pink sign on the edge of the parking lot. Below the club's name, the sign read: LOCAL, ORGANIC FARE. SERVING BREAKFAST, LUNCH AND DINNER.

"An organic menu at a strip club?" Kat glanced at the nondescript double doors.

"I've never been in. I'm not a fan of crowded indoor spaces," Lena said, pulling up to the front door. "But I've heard the food is good."

"If it takes a while to find Josh, maybe I'll see if Brody wants to join me for lunch."

Lena laughed as Kat climbed down from the truck. "Good luck."

Inside, Kat scanned the space. She'd expected a dive, not a classy club serving local eggs and grass-fed bacon. A stage featuring three chrome poles and a long runway commanded the space. Tables with shiny black tops lined the dance floor. Three men sat at one, facing the stage, while a dancer wearing platform heels and a thong lay on top of their table. The woman helped herself to a home fry before turning her attention to the stage. The music shifted to a familiar upbeat song with a bump and grind rhythm. A pair of dancers appeared and began working the poles.

Kat glanced back at the men. Who went to a strip club for breakfast? And where was Brody if he wasn't staring at the stage beside Josh?

A topless waitress brushed past, her breasts bouncing as she slid steaming plates of potatoes and eggs in front of a gentleman. The food smelled so good. Her stomach rumbled as she searched the dimly lit space for Brody and found him by the bar.

Heading over, she noted the way he kept his gaze fixed on the hardwood floor. The tall, broad-shouldered man who liked to lick her until she screamed refused to glance at the strippers.

"If you wanted a lap dance, you could have asked," she said, moving to his side.

Brody looked up, his eyes widening in surprise. "What are you doing here?"

Before she could explain, a twenty-something woman with long black hair approached. She wore a fitted black tank top with pink letters that read Naughty Kitty across her chest, jeans, and black cowboy boots. This was Kat's first visit to a strip club, but nothing about the woman screamed, *Put singles in my underwear.*

"I'm Daphne, the owner," the woman said, offering her hand. "One of the servers mentioned you were looking for someone?"

"Brody Summers." He took her hand. "I'm here for my brother."

Daphne placed her hands on her hips. "Is he under-age?"

"He was in an accident," Kat jumped in, explaining her role as Josh's doctor and her concerns about his possible foray into sexual promiscuity.

The owner, who stood an inch or two shorter than Kat and barely reached Brody's shoulder, laughed. "Josh is in the back."

"In the back?" Brody said. She could feel the tension radiating off him. And right now she couldn't blame him. A back room at a strip club suggested a very intimate dance.

"He's having breakfast with Megan, one of the waitresses. Sweet guy. Drove out here just to keep her company before her shift. I'll let him know you're here." The owner turned and headed for the double doors leading to the kitchen.

"Since you hired a topless waitress to care for your little brother, you shouldn't be too surprised he's sleeping with her," Kat said, taking Brody's hand.

"I didn't know," he ground out. "She's a nursing student. I checked. She's enrolled part-time. And she came highly recommended."

She gave his hand a squeeze. "At least he didn't come for the show."

"If I'd realized sexual promiscuity was a common side effect of head injuries, I would have hired a different nurse. Maybe tried to find a guy."

"It's not your fault, Brody." She glanced at the man who tried to shoulder the weight of everyone's needs.

And she realized it was time someone rescued him right back.

She moved in front of him. "You know, now that we're here, I have to admit, I like the idea of giving you a lap dance."

"No." One arm wrapped around her waist, drawing her back against his chest. In the dimly lit, empty corner of the club, she arched, pressing into him. She felt his hand brushing her hair to one side. His lips touched her neck.

"Might be wild," she said before he gave her a list of reasons why he shouldn't accept a dance from her. "And a little naughty."

She felt him suck in a deep breath, his free hand resting on her shoulder. "Dammit, I missed you. I'm glad you're back."

"Brody, what the fuck?" Josh stormed through the double doors leading to the kitchen, his hands shoved in the front pockets of his jeans. "I left a note. You don't need to follow me around like I'm a freaking child. I know my way home."

Brody stepped to the side, crossing his arms on his chest. "Your note didn't mention Megan. You said you were going to a strip club at nine in the morning on a Friday. I figured maybe you'd lost your common sense too."

"I didn't want you to judge Megan," Josh shot back. "She's trying to pay her school loans. College and nursing school aren't free, and waiting tables here pays well. More than you're paying her."

"I'm not judging," Brody said. "I was worried."

"Well, you can stop. I'm fine," Josh said, his voice rising with every word.

Kat saw a bouncer move in their direction and stepped forward, placing herself between the fuming, stubborn brothers. "Josh, we should sit down and talk."

"You said you'd be around for another week or so, Doc. We have time." He stepped back. "I'm going to finish my food. I'll see you at home later."

"Josh," Brody snapped.

Kat turned to him, placing her hands on his biceps. "How about we stay for breakfast? I'm starving."

"I'm not sitting down here. Not with you."

"I have a feeling you're not leaving without Josh, and seeing as how Lena dropped me off, you're my ride."

She took his arm and pulled him over to a table near the kitchen, away from the stage.

"I didn't get a chance to finish my lunch yesterday. Dinner consisted of chips and animal crackers on the plane. And my flight was late. In another ten minutes I'll be hungry enough to eat my potatoes off a dancer's back like that guy up there." She nodded to the table by the stage.

"What the heck?" He stole a peek before sinking into one of the wooden chairs. "Aren't there rules about touching the dancers?"

"He's not using his hands. Who knows, maybe he asked permission." Kat claimed the seat beside Brody and selected two menus from the stack resting between the napkin holder and the salt. Out of the corner of her eye she saw the bouncer approach the table with the woman lying on top. Maybe there were rules about running your tongue over a stripper's back.

But later, she thought, after they returned from their "rescue" mission and disappeared into Brody's bedroom, there would be nothing stopping him from running his mouth over her.

"See if you can get the waitress's attention," Kat said, brushing his leg under the table. "Let's order. And then you can describe your dream lap dance."

Chapter 16

BRODY HAD SPENT the past twenty-four hours spinning a web of lies. His bed hadn't felt empty without her. He didn't miss her laughter, her smile, or that vulnerable look in her eyes when she revealed a part of her past. And he sure as hell wasn't falling for the sexy, smart doctor.

But then Kat had waltzed in, defused the situation with Josh one moment and teased him with the promise of a lap dance the next. She made him face the fact that he'd been lying to himself since she left. He wanted Kat in his life and in his bed. Falling for her wasn't a question. He was already there at the bottom, hoping like hell she'd follow him.

Maybe it was the way she didn't expect him to solve her problems, or how she rejected his pity, demanding that she feel anything but sorry for her. Either way, he had to make this work. He had to find a way to give her everything she deserved and still honor his commitments here.

One thing she didn't need? A man who landed her in a strip club on a weekday morning. A man who was going out of his mind with desire while watching her eat eggs and potatoes.

Kat wrapped her lips around a forkful of scrambled eggs and closed her eyes. "I think I'm beginning to see the difference between free range eggs and the regular kind. These are amazing. And these home fries."

She punctuated her sentence with a low moan.

Brody shifted in his chair. Hell, even watching her eat turned him on. "Are you sure that's not the hunger talking?"

"No. It's the potatoes." She loaded her fork. "You must come back here. For the food. Though the dancers are talented too."

"I wouldn't know," he said, pushing his full plate toward her. "I can't take my eyes off you."

"I already promised you a private dance." She licked a smear of ketchup off her lower lip. "Now start talking. I want details. Does the no touching rule turn you on?"

"No." With Kat sitting there, torturing him with every movement of her lips, every word, he didn't want to entertain lies. "If anyone is going to be tied up, unable to touch, it's you."

She raised an eyebrow. "You won't hand over control even for a lap dance?"

"Not a chance." He wanted to tie her up and make her *his*. He wanted to claim her. And he didn't want to let go after a few orgasms. He didn't want to come home needing her—her smile, her words, her comfort—and find out she'd slipped away again. And he sure as hell didn't want the woman he cared deeply for returning to a lonely life.

"What's in New York?" he asked. "Why did you need to go back?"

Her teasing smile faded. "Prior commitment."

"Must have been pretty important if you took back-to-back red-eyes and ate animal crackers for dinner."

She set her fork down and whipped her mouth with her napkin. "I joined a mentor program last year and I was matched with a young girl living in foster care. Twice a month I sit down with her for an hour at her elementary school. Eventually I was hoping to do some weekend day trips."

He'd paged through the usual explanations while she was away—a patient who needed her, a doctor's appointment, or the one that drove him to the brink of jealousy, a date. But he'd never pictured her sitting down to lunch with a child who was traveling down the same road she'd taken as a kid.

"Yesterday," she continued, "Brianna opened up."

"You're going to get your weekend adventures?"

Kat smiled, not the teasing grin she used to so effortlessly seduce him or the professional expression she offered others, but a genuine look of joy mingled with excitement.

"Yes. And fingers crossed a lot more. God, I don't want to say too much or I'm afraid I'll jinx it. But Brianna asked if I'd consider adopting her. And I said yes."

"That's great, Kat." But the weight of her words sank

in, leaving him face-to-face with a complicated mess. How would they make this work if she had a family on the other side of the country and his needed him here?

"Brianna deserves to have something good happen for once," Kat said.

"So do you." And he wanted that something good in her life to be him. But Brody had a sinking feeling he was looking at the one person who didn't need him—not nearly as much as he needed her.

"I've been very fortunate, Brody. After all, I went to Harvard," she said, her tone changing to sarcasm.

"That's not what I meant and you know it. You deserve happiness and family. Just like Brianna."

She stabbed the last potatoes on her plate. "I think our conversation took a wrong turn toward serious. And I don't think this is the place."

"You're right." The Lost Kitten strip club wasn't the place to tell her that he wanted to be a part of her future happiness. "But—"

His cell phone cut him off, vibrating against his thigh. Retrieving it, he glanced at the caller ID. Moore Timber. Great. With Eric away on his honeymoon, he couldn't ignore the call.

He stood and headed for the door. "I need to take this. Outside."

As BRODY DISAPPEARED into the daylight beyond The Lost Kitten's timeless interior, Kat helped herself to his potatoes.

"Your boyfriend hasn't taken his eyes off you since you walked in." Daphne, the owner with the long black hair, claimed Brody's empty seat.

"He's not my boyfriend," Kat said, the words quickly snapping the imaginary lines binding her to Brody. But saying those words for the second time since she'd landed back in Oregon this morning—they left her uneasy, as if she was lying.

Daphne's eyebrows shot up. "He stared at your mouth as if he owned it. There were a few times that I swore he was going to push the dishes to the floor and take you here."

"Those looks were your fault," Kat said, reaching for humor. "The food was so good, I thought I'd have an orgasm just from eating the potatoes."

Daphne leaned her head back and laughed. "Can I bring you back to the kitchen before you leave? I need you to repeat those words to my chef. He's going to drop to one knee when he hears that and beg to marry you."

"Sure. But fair warning, if he proposes, I might run for the door."

Brody returned to the table, his intense brown eyes focusing briefly on the club owner before turning to her. He stopped beside her chair, resting a hand on her shoulder. "Everything OK?"

"Great." Kat smiled up at him. "We were just talking potatoes."

Pressing her palms flat against the table, Daphne stood. "I'd still like to steal her away to the kitchen to meet my chef before you leave."

"I'll send her back in a minute." Brody looked down at her. "I need to head out. One of the trucks went off the road near a harvest site. Are you OK to catch a ride back with Josh?"

She placed her hand on his. "I'll make sure your brother gets home."

"Thanks." He released her and withdrew his wallet.

"Breakfast is on me." She stood and guided his hand holding his wallet back to his pocket. Once he'd returned the billfold, she gave his butt a squeeze. "I have an idea about how you can repay me later." She rose up on her tiptoes and touched her lips to his cheek. "Let me dance for you."

"Deal. But I get to touch."

Brody turned and headed for the door, his phone pressed to his ear. She'd never met a man so willing to give—his time, his energy, his support, his everything. And tonight she wanted to give back. The labels might remain out of reach, but there was one place where she could deliver everything she had to give.

"Just you wait, Brody Summers," she murmured as she headed toward the kitchen. "Tonight, you're getting the lap dance to end all lap dances."

Chapter 17

"YOU AND I need to talk," Brody said as he closed the kitchen door and headed for the chairs lining the table. Sitting down, he began unlacing his work boots, his gaze fixed on his brother.

"Yeah, we do." Josh leaned back against the kitchen counter, holding a beer in each hand. His spiral notebook stuck out of his back pocket, but Josh didn't reach for it. "What the hell were you thinking, chasing me to The Lost Kitten?"

"Trying to keep you from doing something stupid," Brody snapped as the first boot hit the floor. "Or getting hurt."

"I'm cleared to drive. I have been for over a month. Just because I can't always remember where I'm headed doesn't mean I don't know how to operate my truck. And Megan was with me."

Brody shook his head. "I can't believe you didn't tell

me I'd hired a topless waitress to take care of you. Or hell, write it on a Post-it note."

"I took it as a sign of love." Josh raised one bottle to his lips and took a long drink. "And she's not working for us anymore," he added. "She's quitting. We planned to tell you today, but you were working."

"You're still seeing her." Brody set his second boot beside his first.

"She's out in the studio apartment right now. I just came in for some refreshments." He held up the bottles. "There's more in the fridge. And you look like you could use one. Or you could just head upstairs. Katie is staying at Liam's house tonight," he added. "I called Chad and told him to clear out too. The place is all yours, and I believe the good doctor is waiting for you in your room." Josh headed for the door. "Feel free to make all the noise you want."

"We're not done here." Brody crossed his arms on his chest. Part of him wanted to race up the stairs, find Kat and lose himself in her. But first he needed to talk to his brother.

"We are for tonight," Josh said, and grinned at him. "Did I mention Megan was waiting for me in the apartment?"

"Yeah, you did."

His brow furrowed as he studied his brother. Something was different. Brody's gaze drifted to the notebook, and the realization damn near knocked the wind out of him.

"You haven't checked your notes once," he said, arms falling to his sides.

Josh looked at the floor, a sheepish grin spreading across his face. "Yeah, about that. My memory has been coming back. Bit by bit."

"And you didn't tell anyone?"

"I told Kat. Or she figured it out."

Your brother is on the road to recovery. He'd been meaning to ask her what she meant by those words.

"I asked her not to tell you," Josh added. "I still feel like I can't quite trust it. You know, like did I get a very special wake-up call from Megan or was that my imagination?"

"Joke all you want," Brody said, closing the space between them and wrapping his arms around his little brother. "I'm just so fucking relieved that Kat's treatment is working."

"I'm not sure that is the reason," Josh said as Brody released him and stepped back. Suddenly starting his day in a room full of strippers—with the only woman he wanted to see naked—didn't seem quite so bad. And so what if he'd spent the remaining hours of daylight in a ditch trying to fix a truck that belonged in the junkyard? The end was looking pretty damn good.

"I think my memory was coming back before she arrived. Doc said it could happen at any time. I didn't trust it, so it really freaked me out. And probably contributed to my depression."

Brody frowned. "Is Kat kicking you out of the trial?"

"She doesn't know for sure yet. We talked about it on the drive back today. She hasn't heard from the lead doctor, but it doesn't sound good. I can keep taking the antidepressant. And she had a few other ideas." Josh hesitated. "But she'll probably be leaving soon. I'm sorry, Brody."

"Don't be. I'll talk to her." He clapped Josh on the arm, the relief still pulsing through him. "And we're here for you. Don't forget that. For as long as it takes. Now go, see Megan."

Josh disappeared into the darkness, the door slamming shut behind him. Brody ran his hands over his face, the relief still seeping in. Tomorrow he could talk to Josh about the long-term. He'd call a family meeting and they'd figure it out together. Right after he met the tow truck to haul the broken-down semi off the side of the logging road. Plus, he needed to sit down with Kat to find out if his brother was officially out of the trial.

And somewhere in there, he should probably tell her that he was falling in love with her. Somewhere between keeping the trucking side of Moore Timber running, taking every search and rescue mission that came his way, and looking out for his family, he needed to ask Kat to stay. Because any way he looked at their relationship, she was his.

His hand on the banister, one foot on the bottom stair, Brody closed his eyes. Maybe he should go up there and have that conversation right now, before they landed back in his bed. It was the right thing to do. Kat deserved to know that he wanted something lasting with her. Settling for less felt plain wrong.

And it would break his heart.

At the top of the stairs he headed for his door. His day,

the crazy rush to find his brother, the call to help with the truck, the knowledge that Josh was getting better, it all faded away as he turned the knob. The need to see Kat, to hold her, rose to the surface.

Stepping into the bedroom he'd lived in for the past thirty-some years, he spotted her on his bed. His gaze ran up her long bare legs to the slip of black lace covering the part of her body he wanted to worship until sunrise, over her belly to her chest. Matching lace cups covered her breasts. In one hand she held a magazine, the pages folded back to reveal a picture of a brain. Her gaze met his and her entire face lit up with an intoxicating mix of need and excitement.

Lying there, waiting for him, she took his fucking breath away. His Little Miss Perfect.

"Some light reading?" he asked.

"*Neurology Today.*" She set the magazine on the night-stand and swung her legs over the edge of the bed, sitting up. "They published my article on new ways to treat athletes suffering from multiple concussions."

"Let me guess, baking?"

She laughed. "That's part of it."

"I hear it works. One of your patients just told me his memory is coming back."

"Josh did? Good. I'm sorry I couldn't say anything."

Brody shook his head. "Don't be. He was your patient. Not me."

"I'm glad we're clear on that," she murmured, rising from the bed. "I had plans for tonight that would be highly inappropriate if I was treating you."

She closed the space between them and rose up on her tiptoes to brush a kiss over his lips. "How was your day, Brody?"

"I woke up missing you in my bed." He held onto her hips, needing to keep her close. "Once I got you back, I had to leave you in a strip club. But then I came home, learned my brother was going to be OK. And then I found you here. In my bed."

"Sounds like a roller-coaster. Lots of ups and downs. Maybe I should help you relax." She placed a hand on his chest, pressing him back. "Are you ready for your private dance? Your brother took his time finishing his breakfast at the club. While I waited, I watched the dancers."

"Oh?" They hadn't captured his attention. But the thought of Kat watching them . . . oh yeah, he liked that mental picture. But then the thought of Kat doing just about anything would probably turn him on. "Did you like what you saw?"

Her hands moved to his biceps, guiding him back until his calves hit the chair. "I learned a few moves."

"I don't give a damn about their moves," he growled, his need rising. Two nights without her in his bed and he was damn near dying to have her. "I want you."

Desire flared in her green eyes. "Sit, Brody."

He obeyed, drawing her down with him. His hands ran up her thighs as she straddled his lap. "I need to touch you," he said.

"It's against the rules. The bouncers were clear on that. Some guy tried to pull one of the dancer's panties off while she was lying across his table and—"

"I'm not some guy, Kat." He palmed her perfect ass, his fingers running over the thin strip of her thong underwear. "I'm yours."

She began to move over him, her hips grinding against his lap. "I'll let the rules slide. This time. On one condition."

"I'm listening."

Leaning forward, her breasts pressed against his chest, her lips touched his ear. "Close your eyes and tell me about your fantasy lap dance."

"Easy."

He captured her mouth, kissing her deeply. Keeping his eyes closed, he broke away as his hands moved up her back to the clasp of her bra. He undid the series of hooks, felt his way to her shoulders and guided the straps down. The bra fell to his lap as he cupped her breasts.

"You," he said, opening his eyes. "You're my fantasy." *And so much more.*

"You have me." Kat's hands pulled at his T-shirt, freeing it from his pants.

His thumbs brushed her nipples. "Good, because I can't let you go."

"Hmm, please don't."

Brody's hands froze. He needed to tell her now. This was so much more than foreplay. "Kat—"

"Lean forward," she ordered, her movements frantic as she drew his shirt over his head. She placed a hand on his shoulder, pressing him back, and reached for his belt.

He had so much to say, but feeling her fingers against

his lower abdomen, unbuttoning his pants, drawing the zipper down . . . She brushed his dick, and his mind zeroed in on one thought.

Take me.

"The dancers at The Lost Kitten, did they strip off their customers' clothes?" he asked.

"No. I'm improving on their model." She shifted off his lap. Standing between his splayed legs, she reached for his waistband. "Lift your hips."

He did as she asked, his pants and underwear joining his shirt in a pile on the floor. Her gaze lingered on his erection for a second before she looked up.

"Don't move, Brody."

Swaying her hips to an imaginary beat, she began to dance. Her fingers toyed with her thong. Slowly, she slid the slip of black lace down her legs and kicked them to the side.

"If you find those later, you can keep them," she said. "As a souvenir."

"I don't want your underwear, Kat. I want you." His fingers dug into the arms of the chair. "And I'm going to want you tomorrow and the day after that."

"Brody," she gasped, running her hands up her naked body, cupping her breasts as she continued to move.

"I want you, Kat." He would never stop saying those words to her. Over and over, he'd make damn sure she opened her eyes every morning feeling wanted—a part of his life and his family.

Releasing her breasts, she placed her hands on his

shoulders and reclaimed his lap. She was wet and hot against his cock and he nearly forgot the words he needed to say before he sank into her.

His hands moved to her hips, holding her still.

"Brody?" She raised an eyebrow, the heat and need in her eyes matching his. He hoped. God, he hoped she felt the same way.

"You deserve so much more, Kat."

She slipped her hand between them, reaching for him. "I'm not sure I could handle any more."

The humor in her tone was like a warning. And a signal that she'd raised her defenses.

"Kat, I need you to listen to me." He kept his gaze locked with hers, watching as wariness displaced desire.

"I thought we agreed to abandon the serious sex," she murmured.

"That's not what I'm asking for. I want to be wild with you, Kat. But you should know where this is going, how I feel about you."

"Is this about the lap dance? Is this your way of regaining the upper hand? If you want control, take it, Brody. Take me."

"This is not just sex," he said. "Not for me. Maybe it started out that way, and heck, I thought I was stretched too thin to add a relationship to my life right now, so I held onto that thought. But I fell for you."

He felt her pulling away, her hands pressing against his chest as her feet scrambled to find the floor. But he couldn't hold back the words.

"Kat, I'm falling in love with you."

Chapter 18

IN HER MIND, the difference between loneliness and love spanned the continental United States. It was like the distinction between New York and Oregon. And right now she didn't want either one. She wanted to make an emergency landing in North Dakota and wait out the storm.

Crossing her arms in front of her bare chest, Kat backed away. How had they gone from "I'll brighten your day with a lap dance" to "I'm falling in love with you"? They'd known each other a week. OK, maybe she'd lusted after him for years. But that didn't mean she *knew* him.

"This was insane." She glanced around the room, searching for her clothes. She found her underwear and slipped them on, followed by her bra and the shirt she'd folded beside his bed. "And you had to tell me now?"

"I know what I feel Kat," Brody said, following her lead and pulling on the clothes she'd stripped off him. "And I'll be damned if I'm going to let you feel unwanted and unworthy of love for another day when that is exactly what I feel for you."

"You can't," she said, the words falling out in spite of the panic cartwheeling through her. "In less than a week?"

Wearing only his jeans, he put his hands on his hips. "I can't love a woman who offers support? Who listens to me? And who drives me crazy with desire?"

"I'm not the only woman in the world willing to experiment with kinky fantasies," she shot back.

"No," he said evenly, his gaze locked with hers. "But you're the only one I want to tie up. The only one I want in my bed covered in whip cream. The only one—"

"You don't know enough about me to love me," she snapped, the panic like a tornado now, threatening to envelop her. "What is my favorite color? My favorite food? What kind of movies do I like to watch? And there is so much I don't know about you."

"I don't give a damn about colors. I like a good burger and the occasional steak. I prefer action flicks, but I'll watch just about anything. I've seen *Cinderella* nearly a hundred times because that was Katie's favorite when she was little. I'd be happy if I never saw another Disney princess movie again," he said, the words coming out hot and fast. "How does knowing any of that help?"

"It matters," she said.

His brown eyes stared at her, dark and possessive. She'd seen a glimmer of *she's mine* in his gaze before, and she should have heeded the warning. She should have left before they'd landed here.

"It matters," she continued, her voice rising with each word, "because I think about the number of people who know those things about me, and I come up with a big fat zero."

Kat shook her head. She'd imagined tonight would lead to raised voices, possibly screaming. But not like this.

His hands fell to his sides. "Look Kat, I don't want to fight with you. But I needed to tell you how I feel. I love you, Kat. I don't care if your favorite color is fuchsia or if you saw *Frozen* a dozen times in the theater. I'd like to learn your favorite things, but knowing won't change how I feel about you. I don't know what that means for the future, for us, but—"

"You told me because you think I'm leaving," she said, the pieces of the puzzle falling into place. "Now that Josh has regained his memory, I'll be heading back to the East Coast."

He cocked his head to one side, studying her. "Aren't you?"

She nodded. Her work was in New York. Brianna was there, waiting for her to provide a forever home. The life she'd built for herself—it was all there.

"I had to say something before I took you back to my bed," he said. "It was the right thing to do."

The truth crystallized in her mind. Brody Summers wanted to do the right thing. He never strayed from that path. And that meant giving her what he thought she needed.

But she'd lived most of her life without love, without anyone wanting her beyond her academic and professional life. And she wasn't about to risk her heart, to open herself to the rejection that would come when their week-long fling fell apart. Because it would hurt ten times as much as the family who hadn't wanted to keep her as a child when Brody told her loved her but couldn't be with her. And that day would come.

But not if she got out first. Not if she left the burning fear that had eclipsed every other emotion—desire, wanting, joy—carry her away from here.

"Doing the right thing just cost you a lap dance," she said, turning to the door.

"I didn't fall for the fantasy, Kat," he said. "I fell for you."

Those words planted a kernel of hope. She wanted to believe him. But in just one week? If it was that easy, if it only took a week to learn to love her, why hadn't it happened before?

Because you run. You started running as a teenager, leaving the families before they gave you up. And you haven't stopped.

The hope withered and died before it grew roots. What if Brody changed his mind? What if the very real obstacles proved to be too much? "It won't work, Brody. Your life and your family are here. And mine are waiting for me in New York."

"It's only a plane flight," Brody said. "We can find a way to make it work."

"No, we can't," she said, biting back the words, *I'm too afraid you'll hurt me if I let you in.*

"Good-bye, Brody."

Chapter 19

"PLEASE TELL ME you have a good reason for dragging us out of bed in the middle of the night," Chad said, sinking into a chair beside Lena. The golden retriever at her feet glanced up at Brody with a look that echoed Chad's words.

"It's seven in the morning," Brody said. "You're scheduled to take the helicopter out to a logging site in a couple of hours. Katie has work. And this couldn't wait." He scanned the tired faces seated at his kitchen table.

"If it is about my ring," his sister said, "I showed it to everyone."

"If this is a family meeting, shouldn't Liam be here too?" Chad said. "Based on that rock, he's one of us now."

"I'm here. Without a ring on my finger," Lena added with a pointed look at Chad.

His brother flashed a charming smile. "But you know it's coming. I'm just waiting for the perfect moment."

Brody jumped in before the conversation dissolved to weddings. "Josh has something he wants to share." He nodded to his little brother seated at the opposite end of the table.

"That's why you pulled me out of bed?" Josh demanded. "I could have e-mailed or sent a text. Instead of leaving Megan asleep in my bed."

"Josh." Brody stared down the length of the table.

"Fine," Josh said, glancing from Chad to Lena to Katie. "My memory is coming back."

Suddenly awake and alert, Katie and Chad fired off questions, demanding to know how he was feeling, if he recalled everything and whether this was a result of the treatment. Josh patiently explained what he could.

"We will find out soon if he still qualifies for the trial," Brody added.

"But it doesn't sound like he needs it," Chad said.

"Which means your doctor will be heading home," his sister said, looking at him.

"Kat is Josh's doctor," Brody pointed out. "Not mine."

"Josh isn't the one who has fallen head over heels for Dr. Katherine Arnold," Katie said.

"Katie, I distinctly remember you telling me to mind my own business when you started seeing Liam."

"I did," his sister agreed, reaching for her coffee mug. "But you hiked out to the cabin where we were staying and busted right in."

"We were worried about you," Brody said.

"And now the tables are turned. It's my turn to worry

about you, Brody." Katie took a sip of coffee and added: "Have you told her how you feel about her?"

"She's leaving," Brody said, his voice firm. Hell, as far as he was concerned, she'd already walked away. Sure, he'd followed her into the hall last night pointing out that she couldn't exactly walk up the gravel drive and hail a cab. Though she'd looked ready to try.

"Do you love her?" his sister challenged.

"Back off, Katie," he growled.

"That's a yes," Chad said. "And I'm betting you told her. So what happened, bro?"

"I told her. Kat spent her entire life alone. I can't imagine what that is like because I've always had you," Brody said, looking around the table at his siblings. "I just wanted her to know that I cared."

"And then what happened?" Kat asked, her expression serious.

"She left," he said.

"You let her go?" Chad demanded. "Just like that?"

"What would you have done?" Brody said, not bothering to mask his frustration. "Follow her and demand that she love me back?"

Chad frowned. "When you put it that way, it sounds a little creepy, you're right."

"And it wouldn't work. Making demands," Lena said. "Give her time. And just keep loving her. Without asking for anything in return."

Brody swore he saw Chad grasp Lena's hand under the table and give it a squeeze.

"Lena's right," Katie said. "You need to prove that you're going to stay in her life. No one else ever has. You need to show her that you will."

"Yeah, man, what the hell are we doing here talking about my memory with the sun barely peeking over the mountains when the woman you love is upstairs?" Josh said, pushing back from the table. "For all I know, I might forget everything again tomorrow. My short-term memory isn't important."

"Yes, it is." Katie stood and wrapped her arms around her brother. "I didn't want to start planning my wedding until we knew if there was a chance you'd get your memory back. I'd hoped you would remember the day."

"No guarantees," Josh said.

Brody watched his family exchange hugs and then head for the door. He'd do anything for these people. He'd known that for a long time. And he wanted to add Kat to that group. But he couldn't push her to feel something when she wasn't ready. His family was right. He needed to give her time. And even then there were no guarantees.

But waiting didn't mean he had to avoid her. He could go to her now. And heck, maybe find out her favorite color before she flew across the country.

After taking the stairs two at a time, Brody reached the door to his little sister's childhood room and paused. Inside, he heard Kat's voice. He picked out the words "I understand" and "good-bye." There was a beat of silence and he raised his hand to knock.

And then sobbing.

He froze, recognizing the choked-up gasping for air that accompanied free flowing tears. He'd held his sister while she wept after their father died. In the aftermath of Josh's accident, he'd stood on the other side of the hospital door waiting for his brother's tears to fade, knowing Josh wouldn't want an audience while he cried.

Brody knew the sounds. But he didn't know if Kat wanted comfort or if crying in front of others embarrassed her.

You don't know enough about me to love me.

In the moment, he'd wanted to tell her that love didn't have strict standards. There wasn't a numbered checklist floating around that demanded he know X, Y, and Z before offering his heart. He knew that her compassion drove him nearly as wild as her Miss Perfect looks. And he was in awe of her drive to succeed.

Standing out here, listening to her cry, he had to admit there were things he didn't know. But he knew she'd stood by him when he was feeling ripped apart by a lost kid on a mountain. She didn't need to know his favorite color before offering comfort.

Taking a chance, he raised his hand and knocked. "Kat, it's Brody. Can I—"

"Just a minute," she called, her voice wavering. He heard a deep breath, as if she was struggling to hold back tears.

The door opened. With one hand on the knob, Kat faced him, tears still flowing over her cheeks. But apart from her red eyes, she looked damn near perfect. Wearing the same shirt he'd used to bind her hands that first night in the hotel, a skirt that hugged her curves, and boots, every inch of her screamed "City doctor."

"Just the person I needed to see." Kat forced a smile, her eyes brimming with tears.

"Kat," he said gently, wishing he could wrap his arms around her. But the tension flowing from her, filling the space between them like an imaginary barricade, sent a clear message. *Stand Back!* He had a feeling if he reached for her, she'd break away.

"What happened?" he asked.

"I didn't get her," she said. "Brianna, the little girl who asked me if I would adopt her."

"They said no? To you?" Shock filled his voice. "You would be a great parent. And you know better than anyone what she is going through. I thought the goal was to get kids out of foster care."

"It is. And Brianna is getting a forever home. Just not with me. The family who adopted Brianna's younger sister found out about her and offered to take Brianna too. The state always tries to keep siblings together when they can. And it's the best thing for her." Her voice wavered over the words. "But I had already started to think about her as mine."

Kat's grip tightening on the doorknob, she sucked in a deep, shaky breath. "I was going to make the second bedroom hers. Paint the walls her favorite color. I thought we could turn my apartment into a home. Together."

He reached out and took her hand, his heart breaking

for her. "You can still do that. There are a lot of children out there who need a home."

"I know." Kat closed her eyes, tipping her head back. "Logically, it makes sense. But I wanted quiet, sullen Briana. I thought . . . I thought we could help each other."

One more person ripped out of her life. She'd taken a risk, opening herself to the idea of caring for that little girl. And it had been taken away from her.

Part of him wanted to shout, *I want to build a home with you. And heck, I want to love you.*

"There's more," she said. "When the social worker called, I was on the other line with Dr. Westbury."

"Josh is out, isn't he?"

She nodded. "I'm sorry."

"Don't be. We had a family meeting this morning. We're all so damn grateful his memory is coming back that it doesn't matter if he's part of the trial. I'll make sure he stays on the meds and follows your instructions—"

"I'm leaving, Brody."

Leaving. That one word cut into him. The thought of her alone and hurting on the other side of the country . . .

His jaw tightened. One more tear and he'd scoop her up, carrying her back to his room.

I want to take care of you. Erase your pain.

"Kat." But what could he say that would make her stay? He'd told her how he felt about her last night. And the words had pushed her away. She needed proof. He had to show her, dammit.

"I called a cab company in Salem," she said, stepping back into the room.

"I can drive you," he said, the words straddling the line between command and straight up begging to spend more time with her.

"The driver is on his way." Her green eyes locked with his and he saw a flash of wanting so heartbreaking it tore at him. It was as if he was staring into the eyes of the little girl who'd walking into the Falls Hotel and had her hopes crushed.

And now she was leaving again. Alone. He'd never felt so powerless to help someone he cared about.

"Stay. One more day, Kat. Don't leave like this," he said. "Let me help you."

"You don't need to worry about me. I'll be fine, Brody." She drew the door closed, disappearing behind the wooden barrier.

Brody rested one hand on the wood. "Yes, I do need to worry about you. I love you, Kat," he murmured. "And I'm going to do whatever it takes to prove it to you."

KAT STARED OUT the window, watching the familiar sights of Independence Falls slip away. The driver stopped at a red light in front of A Slice of Independence, and a pang of regret joined her in the cab's backseat. There were so many new places along Main Street that she hadn't explored yet. She'd walked into town determined to hold the past against this place. She'd opened up to the people—more than she'd planned. But she stopped short of looking around this quaint small town set against breathtaking mountains and acknowledging that Independence Falls had changed.

The light turned green and the cab sped down the two-lane road, leaving the downtown in the background. It might be beautiful and new in many ways, but she still couldn't escape the feeling that this place hated her. And today it felt as if Independence Falls was determined to prove it, saddling her with one rejection after another.

Well screw you Oregon, she thought. This time I'm not coming back.

Kat closed her eyes, and a mental image of Brody holding the cab door open, leaning down and looking her in the eyes, appeared. His last words—*I meant what I said last night, Kat. I'm in love with you and I want you in my life*—echoed in her mind. The regret snuggled in, wrapping around her like an old friend.

Opening her eyes, she stared out at wide-open spaces sprinkled with farmhouses. After all these years, she should feel at home with loneliness. But knowing that she was moving farther and farther away from Brody, that Brianna wasn't part of her future in New York . . . For the first time since she'd left for college, her vision of her future appeared bleak.

I wonder what Brody's looks like?

Filled with family and work he loved. Her bottom lip trembled. It was like driving away from every home she'd ever lived in growing up. The people who stayed still had each other. And she was alone.

Except this time the choice was hers.

What if she'd made the wrong one? What if her one chance at love and family was behind her in a dilapidated farmhouse on the outskirts of Independence Falls?

Impossible. The numbers didn't add up. It took more than a few days to find a love that would last forever. And she'd already had her fill of fleeting feelings.

TWENTY-FOUR HOURS LATER Kat stared at her bedroom ceiling wishing for jet lag. She wanted to disappear into sleep, leaving her empty apartment behind. This space—her space—had never felt so lonely.

It's your own fault for picturing Brianna in the spare bedroom.

Pushing that thought away before the tears started flowing again, she closed her eyes and focused on the familiar sounds outside her window. Taxicabs honked and sirens echoed against the tall buildings. But the noise felt distant, so unlike the warm, bustling feeling of the Summers family farmhouse. There was always someone coming or going, the door slamming behind the siblings as they moved through the large kitchen.

"I don't miss the noise," she said, throwing back the bedding in disgust. When she'd first moved to this apartment, she had loved the quiet, empty space. And the fact that it was all hers. After sharing other people's bedrooms and living in dorms during her long years in school, she'd craved space.

She'd wanted this life. She'd worked so hard to build it.

And now it felt empty.

The wall-mounted phone in the hall rang, interrupting her pity party. Grateful for the interruption, even if it was the doorman mistakenly calling her apartment to let her know the neighbors' food delivery had arrived, she raced to the hall.

"Dr. Arnold?" the doorman said. "Brody Summers is here."

"What?" Kat leaned her back against the wall, the phone cord wrapping around her front. "Brody is here?"

"Yes." The doorman hesitated. "Should I send him up?"

Her back ran against the wall as she sank to the ground, still clutching the phone. It wasn't possible. No one had ever come after her. Foster parents, friends, the men she'd casually dated—they'd all let her go, allowing her to gather her fears and run away.

Everyone except Brody Summers.

Kat stared at her bare legs in shock. Brody Summers had flown across the country to see her.

"Dr. Arnold?" the doorman said, his tone uneasy. "I can send him away—"

"No." Kat scrambled to her feet, picturing her sixty-something doorman eyeing tall, broad-shouldered Brody and wondering how he was going to get him out of the building lobby. "Send him up."

"He's on his way."

Of course. Brody had probably headed for the elevators the moment her doorman revealed her floor number. Kat dropped the phone and raced to her front door. Hand on the knob, she glanced down at her gray tank top and underwear.

A knock sounded on the door. "Kat?" Brody's deep voice reached through metal barrier. She turned the dead bolt and cracked the door open.

Brody. Seeing him standing in her hall, filling her doorway with his I-can-save-you muscles, her hope rose up, thrusting her fears aside. His intense brown eyes met hers through the narrowing opening.

"You're here," she said, unable to mask the awe in her voice. "In New York."

"I took the red-eye." He smiled, but the intensity in his brown eyes didn't falter. Not for a second. She saw the wanting, and the relief, as if he'd been counting down the minutes until he could see her again.

He rested one hand on her door frame. The other held a small duffel. "Are you going to let me in?"

"I don't have any pants on," she said.

"Good," he said. "I've been picturing you without them for the last six hours. It made the flight damn uncomfortable."

"I can imagine."

"Let me in, Kat."

Stepping back, she opened the door. Brody stepped into her narrow hallway, dropped his duffel on the floor and gathered her in his arms. And just like that the loneliness that had permeated her apartment since she'd arrived home slipped away.

"I can't believe you're here," she murmured, her hands wrapping around his powerful biceps as if she needed solid proof that he wasn't a figment of her imagination. "Why are you here?"

"I missed you."

She blinked, her mind quickly calculating the hours. "But it has only been—"

His mouth claimed hers, momentarily silencing the internal calculations.

Brody drew back, his forehead touching hers. "I missed you, Kat."

"So you flew across the country?" The disbelief seeped back in as the shock faded. "Just to see me? How long are you staying?"

Lowering his mouth, he glided his tongue over her, tasting her. "I don't know yet. A few nights. I couldn't escape the thought of you here alone."

Her body stiffened, her back pressing against the door. "You flew across the country to save me from being lonely?"

Brody stepped back, offering space as if he could sense her old fears rushing in from all sides. But he kept his gaze fixed on hers. "After you left, I got called out to rescue a hiker with a sprained ankle. The entire time I was out there doing the work I love, carrying that woman down the trail, I thought of you."

Kat crossed her arms in front of her chest, wishing she'd told the doorman to keep Brody downstairs while she put on pants. She wanted to tell him that she hadn't been wallowing in loneliness. But that would be a lie.

"You don't need to save me, Brody." And that was the truth. She would have found a way through on her own. She always did.

"No, I don't," he said. "I didn't drop everything and race to the airport as soon as the hiker was on her way to the hospital because I thought you needed someone. I came because I love you, Kat. And I'll do whatever it takes to prove it to you."

You're here. Kat pressed her lips together. She wished she could say that was enough. But she'd spent years building her defenses. Even if she wanted to let him in, even if she wanted to love him, she couldn't tear the walls down just like that.

"I'm glad you came," she said, lowering her arms and taking a step back.

Brody smiled. "Straight from one helluva long hike. I drew a few stares when I landed in New York wearing muddy work boots and dirty jeans."

She let out a laugh, allowing the weighed emotions, the ones that pushed her toward panic and a flashing, neon exit sign, to fade into the background. For now. "It wasn't your boots, Brody. It's you. But before I take you out and show you the sights, I know just what you need."

He closed the space between them, placing one hand on either side of her head. "Tell me."

"Right now I'm picturing you in my shower, water rushing down your back as I wash every inch of you." Kat ducked under his arm and headed for the hall. Glancing over her shoulder, she smiled back at him. "Does that line up with you mental image?"

"No, Kat," he said, his voice a low growl. "It's better."

BRODY TRIED NEVER to make the same mistake twice. And walking away from a naked woman he'd fallen in love with, a second time, was flat out dumb. He had a plan to prove his feelings for her. As far as he was concerned, it started here, in her shower.

Stripping off his clothes and dropping them beside the panties and shirt she'd abandoned the minute they'd walked into the bathroom, Brody pulled aside the curtain. Little Miss Perfect stood under the shower's warm spray, her head tipped back. Long wet blond hair ran down her back. Her hands moved over her body leaving a trail of bubbles over her breasts. The blood abandoned his brain, racing to his lower body. But he remembered his questions.

"Before I get in, I need to know your favorite color," he said.

Kat stepped out from under the water and wiped her eyes, blinking them open. Her gaze roamed over his naked body, her lips curling up in a soft smile.

Keep looking, Kat. I'm yours, today, tomorrow, and the day after that.

"Pink," she said, her voice teasing his senses, tempting him to reach out and touch her.

Brody climbed in, drawing the shower curtain closed behind him. Wrapping his arms around her, he backed her up against the shower's marble wall, the water rushing over them. He pressed one leg between hers, pinning her in place.

"What about my favorite food?" she asked, her hands moving over his back, drifting up to his shoulders.

"That can wait."

He captured her lips, kissing her, exploring her mouth until she arched. She pressed her breasts against him as if she needed to feel her body against his. Her hands moved to his hair, grabbing on as if she might fight for control. Holding her against the shower wall with his body, careful not to push her against the hot and cold knobs, he wrapped his hands around her wrists and drew them away.

"Wait for what?" she murmured, breaking the kiss as he pinned her arms to the tiles and held them there.

"My next visit."

She stilled, every inch of her frozen. "Planning a lot of trips on the red-eye?"

"Yes. We're not over, Kat." He drew his thigh up, drawing her legs apart. "I'm not asking you for words or promises. All I'm asking is that you don't shut me out. I'm flying out here every damn weekend if that is what it takes to prove to you that my feelings are real and lasting."

"Your brothers and sister," she gasped as he rocked his thigh against her. She adjusted her feet, spreading her legs farther and offering him access. "And your job. What about the trucks? The search and rescue squad?"

"The trucks will survive. And my siblings can live

without me for a weekend. Probably longer at this point." His leg stopped moving as he looked down into her green eyes, wanting her to hear his words. "Chad has Lena now. Katie is marrying Liam. Josh has regained his memory, and I think Megan will be around for a while too. I've been so focused on taking care of them, I didn't think to step back and ask if they really need me."

"They're your family," she said, her eyes wide despite the water falling over them, warming their bodies.

"I'm not cutting them out of my life, Kat. But now that they've moved out and we've sold the business, they don't need me there, holding everything together. I can visit you without my family or my job falling apart. And there are plenty of guys on the search and rescue squad to handle the calls."

"But you love it," she said. "Saving people."

"It's not the only thing I love," he said, hoping like the hell she wouldn't leap out of the shower when that word crossed his lips.

"Brody," she said, her body drawing away from him in spite of his intimate hold on her.

"I want you, Kat. Please don't shut me out. I swear I want you. Just you." Brody drew his thigh away, shifting closer. "And right now, I want to make you scream my name."

KAT CLOSED HER eyes, losing herself in the feel of his lips on her wet skin, kissing her neck. His hands held her wrists above her head, demanding control. With the water rushing over her skin, falling between them, she let him take her. She wanted Brody just the way he was.

Giving.

Caring.

And hard. His hips rocked forward, his cock gliding over her wet skin.

"Condom," she murmured, his lips moving lower, his tongue licking a path across the top of her breasts.

He shifted, capturing both of her wrists in one hand. His free arm shot out, pushing aside the curtain and grabbing a packet from beside the sink.

"You thought ahead."

"I'm not going to lie, Kat." He released her wrists. The intensity of his gaze demanded that she keep her arms against the wall. And she obeyed. "I've stood in the shower dreaming about you, wanting you here with me."

"Tell me," she challenged. "Tell me what you imagined in your daydreams."

He stepped back, placing the length of the tub between them. Standing out of the shower's spray, he tore open the condom and tossed the wrapper onto the floor outside the curtain. One hand wrapped about his hard length, drawing her gaze to the part of his body that she wanted inside her . . .

She gasped as he stroked up and down, her legs threatening to give out beneath her.

"I pictured lifting you up," he said. The rough raw edge in his voice left no doubt that he was coming for her. "Wrapping your legs around me, holding you against the wall while I slid inside. "Just for a moment," he added, his hand moving faster now, up and down, his hips thrusting into his touch.

"And then?"

"I'd release you." He rolled the condom on but remained on the far side of the tub. "I'd tell you to turn around and place your palms against the tiles."

She lowered her arms and followed his instructions, her nipples touching the shower wall, her hands flat. Glancing over her shoulder, she murmured, "Like this?"

He stepped forward, reaching for her hips, his fingers pressing into her skin. Her feet shifted, adjusting her stance as he pulled her toward him. Water rushed over her back, pooling on the center of the flat surface before running over her sides.

"Like this," he said, his fingers touching her, testing her before he slid inside.

Brody groaned and she closed her eyes as he began to thrust against her.

Possessive. She wanted him just like this, taking what he wanted and offering her a sinfully delicious reward.

"Take me, Brody." She screamed the words over and over as he filled her again and again. Holding her hip with one hand, the other slid around her body, his thumb pressing her there, right where she needed him, and pushing her over the edge.

"You're mine," he said as the orgasm took everything she had.

He thrust into her one last time and his hips stilled, holding there, his breath ragged. Slowly, he slid out of her, his hands moving up her body, drawing her back to his front. He wrapped his arms around her, one powerful forearm covering her breasts and the other holding her waist. Warm water washed over her front as his lips brushed her ear.

"You're mine, Kat," he murmured. "I need you so damn much."

I need you too, she thought. She needed the man who understood how much losing a child that had never been hers hurt. The man who would set aside his desire for a lap dance because he had to share his feelings. She needed the man who said the words "you're mine" but also meant "I'm yours."

But need didn't erase the past, offering her a clean slate, even if she wished it would.

"I love you, Kat," he added.

Turning in his arms, she ran her hands up his chest, her gaze following her touch. She couldn't say those three little words. But she was starting to wonder if she felt them for this man who'd come after her, determined to fight for a place in her life. And if she did, would love erase her fears?

"I love you, Kat," he said again, silencing her internal debate. "And I plan to be here next weekend and the one after that, telling you over and over. I want you in my life, Kat. And I'll say the words over and over until you feel them in your heart."

Chapter 21

"I CAN'T COME this weekend."

Brody said the words and Kat's emotions went into a tailspin. After five weekends together—three spent in Manhattan, one in Nebraska where she'd met with a patient, and another in Portland—time had run out.

Dammit, she'd known this would happen. One day he'd wake up and realize he didn't want her anymore. The distance was too much. His family needed him. There would be a logical list of reasons to set aside the words that came so easily to him.

She closed her eyes, shutting out the view of Central Park beyond her bedroom window. "I understand, Brody," she said into her cell. "It's a long trip and we've only known each other—"

"I'm coming back, you know that, right?" he said. "You're not worried . . . Kat, I'm not giving up on you. My sister decided to get married on Saturday. I need to be here to walk her down the aisle. You're welcome to fly out. I want you here, Kat. And so does my sister. But I know you've been busy at work. And hell, this is last minute."

The relief left her dizzy and she sank to the floor, her hand on the window "You're asking me to crash another wedding?"

"Not crash, Kat. This one is friends and family only. And as far as I'm concerned, you're family."

A door slammed in the background and three people—Katie, Josh, and Chad—all started speaking at once.

"Look Kat, I can't talk now. Just because Katie decided on a last minute wedding under her trees doesn't mean it is going to be a simple affair."

Kat suspected those last words were only partially for her.

"But if you can make the trip let me know," Brody continued. "And I'll find a way to pick you up at the airport. If not, I'll see you the following weekend in New York. I'll be there. You have my word."

And Brody kept his promises—in bed and out.

"I'll see what I can do," she said as his sister's voice rose in the background. "Good luck Brody."

And I love you.

She dropped the phone before the words escaped. But she knew what was in her heart. She'd moved past crush to head-over-heels in love with Brody Summers. She'd known for a while, she'd simply been too scared to accept the truth. She'd feared the end would sneak up on her the moment she said those words. Opening her heart, offering him the power to break it to pieces if he walked away, it terrified her.

But Brody Summers kept coming back. For six weeks he'd traveled to be with her. And he would keep flying back and forth across the country, or meeting her in the middle of Nowhere USA if she asked. This man loved her. And he would always return to her.

Brody had labeled her family. In his world, that word was entrenched in commitment. And she was finally willing to open herself up to the possibility that maybe love and family would last this time. They'd hit the 457 day mark and just keep going.

Tears flowed and joy mixed with relief. The love of her life wanted her, today, tomorrow, and the day after. She stared out at Central Park's manicured trees. New York had given her so much, but her heart was in the wild woods of Independence Falls.

"I need to crash that wedding."

"It's a nice day. Clear sky and the sun is out," Brody said, staring out at the Cascade Mountains. If he looked at the pacing crazy woman who'd replaced his sister, the words "calm down" would escape. And then she'd try to bite his head off again. He glanced at the half-dozen people gathered in the clearing by the trees.

Josh stood with his arm around Megan. Beside them, Chad held tight to Lena and Hero, her service dog curled at her feet. To Lena's right, Eric stood beside Georgia, who maintained a tight hold on Nate. The four-year-old kept eyeing the construction equipment resting beside Katie and Liam's future home site. Even though work had begun on the foundation, his sister had insisted they hold the wedding here. And on this perfect Oregon day, it seemed like a good idea. And the people that mattered—his family—were all here.

Except for Kat.

"I swear, if you mention the weather one more time," his sister said, pacing at the edge of the woods. "I'm going to—"

The sound of a car bumping down the dirt road leading to the clearing cut Katie off. Brody turned and spotted a cab that looked as if it belonged at the Portland airport, not out in the middle of nowhere.

"What the hell," Katie said.

The door opened and out tumbled the woman he loved. She pulled her fancy, oversized suitcase out of the backseat, swept a few errant strands of blond hair out of her eyes, and headed toward them without even a glance at the group gathered by the trees.

"Kat?" He met her halfway, easily covering the distance between the edge of the clearing and the driveway. Behind him, he heard the rustle of satin or chiffon or whatever the hell his sister had chosen for her dress.

"I'm sorry," Kat said, drawing the suitcase to a stop. "The traffic was awful. Am I too late?"

The familiar sound of the bridal march blasted from the speakers they had set up the day before. Brody looked down the pair of fir trees. "No, but—"

"Stop the music!" His sister screamed.

"Katie—"

"Dr. Katherine Arnold's here," Katie called like a

herald proclaiming the queen's arrival. But there was a hint of mischief in her bellowing voice. "She'll be down in a few minutes and then we'll start."

"Katie." Liam's voice held a world of warning.

"I'll be there, Liam. I promise. " His sister turned to him. "You have five minutes. Five. So don't go crazy."

His sister headed back to the spot she'd insisted was the proper place to start her walk down the "aisle," and Brody turned to Kat. The clock was ticking. There was so much he wanted to say.

"You're here," he said. "Why didn't you call? I would have picked you up. When did you get to Portland?"

"I arrived this morning." She smiled up at him. "I took the red-eye."

"You flew all night in an evening gown?" he said, surprise dragging him away from the right words. She was here, in Oregon, with his family. He didn't care if she wore jeans to the wedding. Though he had to admit, he liked the strapless neckline pressing against the swell of her breasts. And the way the fitted pale blue dress hugged her curves.

Five minutes. He had five minutes.

"If I'm going to crash another wedding, I wanted to at least be dressed for it," she said.

"You're not crashing. You were invited." *You belong here.* "And I'm damn glad you decided to say yes."

Brody drew her into his arms, his lips claiming hers, kissing her deeply, thoroughly.

"Two minutes!" Katie called.

Breaking away, he stared down at her. He had a feeling his smile matched hers. "I want more, but it will have to wait until after the ceremony. After my sister says her vows, we can sneak away. Thank you for being here. I don't know what you had to do to make it happen, but I appreciate it." His lips brushed hers, stealing one last kiss. "How long are you staying?"

"Forever."

BRODY'S EYES WIDENED. Beaming up at him, Kat broke free from his hold and gave him a gentle push toward his sister.

"Go," she said. "Walk your sister down the aisle. I'll not leaving, Brody. I promise."

Abandoning her suitcase by the driveway, Kat ran, as fast as she could in heels on the soft Oregon dirt, to where her Independence Falls family stood by the pair of fir trees. Claiming a spot beside Lena, she turned and watched the man she loved lead his sister across the grassy field to her happily ever after.

At the end of their long walk, Katie Summers kissed her brother's cheek before turning to Liam. And Brody glanced back at her, his deep brown eyes filled with hope and love. Excitement bubbled up. But she'd waited three days to tell Brody what was in her heart. She could wait until the judge standing under the fir trees declared Katie and Liam husband and wife.

After the bride and groom said their vows—Liam promising to always take in Katie's goats and let her make her own choices, and Katie promising to love him madly even if he one day decided thirty horses was one too many—the bride tossed her bouquet of hand-tied wild-flowers to the ground. Throwing her arms around Liam's neck, she kissed him, long and hard.

"Someone told her that she has to keep her clothes on until after the reception, right?" Chad murmured from the other side of Lena.

"I don't think that's a rule," Lena said with a laugh as the bride reluctantly loosened her hold on the groom and turned to face her family.

So much happiness, Kat thought.

Brody caught her attention, his intense gaze narrowing in on her as he abandoned the happy couple who'd returned to kissing under the trees.

And that is what I want with you Brody Summers. I'm ready. Finally.

The man she loved appeared at her side and claimed her hand. "Come with me."

"We can't leave the wedding," she protested, glancing back at his brothers, who'd clearly noted their abrupt departure and were probably already planning ways to give Brody grief later.

"I'll have you back before the buffet," he growled, drawing her past the tree line and into the forest.

"There's a buffet?" she murmured.

"It's all soy meat so don't too excited," he said, turning her back to the clearing. He guided her one step and then another until she felt a tree trunk press against her back.

"I'm excited, Brody." She reached for him, running

her hands up his arms, needing to touch him. "But not for the food. I want you. Only you."

His hands pinned her hips to the tree, his gaze darting to her lips. "I'll tell you mine if you tell me yours," he challenged.

"My vision for how this plays out?"

He moved closer, his chest touching her as her hands ran up his shoulders, over his neck, weaving through his short brown hair. "Your mental picture for our future, Kat. What did you mean when you said forever?"

She met his questioning gaze. "I want to spend tomorrow with you and the day after that. I'm staying here in Independence Falls. With you."

"But your job?"

"I'll make it work, Brody. I'm one of the best in the country. I'll find something. You know, they have hospitals here too."

"You're staying." She felt the tension rising, every muscle in his body waiting for confirmation.

"I finally found my place, Brody. I'm no longer afraid to say it is right here, with you." She rose up, brushing her lips over his. "And I have this feeling that you're not walking away."

"Never, Kat. I swear—"

"I love you, Brody." She cupped his face, staring into his eyes. Saying those words—there was no fear, only hope for a future she'd never thought possible and a love that exceeded her fantasies. "And I want to spend the rest of my days with you, and my nights in your bed. I want to be wild with you, Brody Summers. Forever."

The World of Sara Jane Stone
Don't miss the rest of Sara Jane Stone's
thrilling Independence Falls novels!
Available now from Avon Impulse

Full Exposure

Book One: Independence Falls

No touching allowed...

After serving her country, Georgia Trulane craves adventure—and sex. She's set her sights on her brother's best friend, now her boss since she took a temporary job as his nephew's live-in nanny. Only problem? Eric refuses to touch her. That doesn't stop Georgia from seducing him. But an earth-shattering encounter leaves Georgia fully exposed, body and soul.

Eric has a long list of reasons to steer clear of the woman he has wanted for as long as he can remember. For one, he refuses to be her next thrill ride. When he claims her, it will be for good. But the attraction is undeniable, and the more they fight it, the stronger it pulls. But will it be enough to conquer their obstacles?

Full Exposure

Book One: Independence Falls

No touching allowed...

After serving her country, Georgia Trulane craves adventure—and sex, but—eventure. She's set her sights on her brother's best friend, now her boss since she took a temporary job as his nephew's live-in nanny. Only problem? Eric refuses to touch her. That doesn't stop Georgia from seducing him. But an earth-shattering encounter leaves Georgia fully exposed, body and soul...

Eric has a long list of reasons to steer clear of the woman he has wanted for as long as he can remember. For one, he refuses to be her next thrill ride. When he claims her, it will be for good. But the attraction is undeniable, and the more they fight it, the stronger it pulls. But will it be enough to conquer their obstacles?

Caught in the Act

Book Two: Independence Falls

*Falling for his rivals' little sister
could cost him everything. . .*

For Liam Trulane, failure is not an option. He
is determined to win a place in Katie Summers's
life before she leaves Independence Falls for
good. But first he needs to make amends
for the last time they got down and dirty.

Only problem?

His professional success hinges on striking a
deal to buy Katie's family business. And after
Liam's relationship with their Katie went south
years ago, the Summers brothers are more
enemies than friends. If both parties agree to
set the past aside, they can close the deal. But
when Katie welcomes him back into her bed,
Liam risks everything to make Katie *his*. . .

After Liam betrayed her trust, Katie Summers will do anything to keep him from walking away with the family business. She decides to seduce Liam, knowing that when her brothers find out, they will back off from the deal. And she'll finally have her revenge. But when her plan spirals out of control, Katie learns that payback might come at too high a price . . .

Hero By Night

Book Three: Independence Falls

Armed with a golden retriever and a concealed
weapons permit, Lena Clark is fighting for
normal. She served her country, but the
experience left her emotionally numb and
estranged from her career-military family.
Staying in Independence Falls seems like
the first step to reclaiming her life until the
town playboy stumbles into her bed . . .

Chad Summers is living his dream—helicopter
logging by day and slipping between the
sheets with Mrs. Right Now by night. Until
his wild nights threaten his day job, leaving
Chad with a choice: prove he can settle down
or kiss his dream good-bye. But when he
ends up in the wrong bed, the one woman
in Independence Falls he can't touch offers
a tempting proposition. Chad is ready and
willing to give in to the primal desire to make

Lena his at night—on one condition. By day, they pretend their relationship is real.

But their connection extends beyond the bedroom, threatening to turn their sham into reality, if Chad can prove he's the hero Lena needs night and day . . . forever.

About the Author

After several years on the other side of the publishing industry, **SARA JANE STONE** bid good-bye to her sales career to pursue her dream-writing romance novels. Sara Jane currently resides in Brooklyn, New York, with her very supportive real-life hero, two lively young children and a lazy Burmese cat. Visit her online at www.sarajanestone.com or find her on Facebook at Sara Jane Stone.

Join Sara Jane's newsletter to receive new release information, news about contests, giveaways, and more! To subscribe, visit www.sarajanestone.com and look for her newsletter entry form.

Discover great authors, exclusive offers, and more at hc.com

Give in to your impulses . . .
Read on for a sneak peek at four brand-new
e-book original tales of romance
from HarperCollins.
Available now wherever e-books are sold.

CHANGING EVERYTHING
A Forgiving Lies Novella
By Molly McAdams

CHASE ME
A Broke and Beautiful Novel
By Tessa Bailey

YOURS TO HOLD
Ribbon Ridge Book Two
By Darcy Burke

THE ELUSIVE LORD EVERHART
The Rakes of Fallow Hall Series
By Vivienne Lorret

An Excerpt from

CHANGING EVERYTHING
A Forgiving Lies Novella
by Molly McAdams

Paisley Morro has been in love with Eli Jenkins
since they were thirteen years old. But after
twelve years of being only his best friend and
wingman, the heartache that comes from
watching him with countless other women
becomes too much, and Paisley decides it's
time to lay all her feelings on the table.

Paisley

I fidgeted with my coffee cup as I tried to find the courage to say what I'd held back for so long. Twelve years. Twelve years of waiting, hoping, and aching were about to come to an end. With a deep breath in, I looked up into the blue eyes of my best friend, Eli, and tensed my body as I began.

"This guy I met, Brett, he's—well, he's different. Like, he's a game changer for me. I look at him, and I have no doubt of that. I have no doubt that I *could* spend the rest of my life with him." I laughed uneasily and shrugged. "And I know that sounds crazy after only a few weeks, but, honestly, I knew it the first day I met him. I don't know how to explain it. It wasn't like the world stopped turning or anything, there was just a feeling I had." Swallowing past the tightness in my throat, I glanced away for a moment as I strained to hold on to the courage I'd been building up all week. "But there's this other guy, and I swear this guy owns my soul."

Eli crossed his arms and his eyebrows rose, but I didn't allow myself to decipher what his expression could mean at that moment. If I tried to understand him—like I always did—then I would quickly talk myself out of saying the words I'd been thinking for far too long.

"Eli," I whispered so low the word was almost lost in the chatter from the other people in the coffee shop. "I have been in love with you since I was thirteen years old," I confessed, and held my breath as I waited for any kind of response from him.

Nothing about him changed for a few seconds until suddenly his face lost all emotion. But it was there in his eyes, like it always was: denial, confusion, shock.

I wanted to run, but I forced myself to blurt out the rest. "I've kept quiet for twelve years, and I would've continued to if I hadn't met Brett. These last few weeks have been casual, but I know he wants it to be more. But if there is a chance of an us, then there would be absolutely no thoughts of anything else with him."

Eli just continued to stare at me like I'd blown his mind, and my body began shaking as I silently begged him to say something—anything.

After twelve years of being his best friend, of being used by him as a shield from other women, of being tortured by his pretending touches and kisses . . . I was slowly giving up on us. I couldn't handle the heartache anymore. I couldn't stand being unknowingly rejected again and again. I couldn't continue being his favorite person in the world for an entirely different reason than he was mine. I couldn't keep waiting around for Eli Jenkins.

This was it for me.

"Eli, I need to know." I exhaled softly and tried to steady my shaking as I asked, "Is there *any* possibility of there being an us?"

An Excerpt from

CHASE ME
A Broke and Beautiful Novel
by Tessa Bailey

Bestselling author Tessa Bailey launches the
Broke and Beautiful trilogy, a fun and sexy
New Adult series set in New York City!

Roxy Cumberland's footsteps echoed off the smooth, cream-colored walls of the hallway, high heels clicking along the polished marble. When she caught her reflection in the pristine window overlooking Stanton Street, she winced. This pink bunny costume wasn't doing shit for her skin tone. A withering sigh escaped her as she tugged the plastic mask back into place.

Singing telegrams still existed. Who knew? She'd actually laughed upon seeing the tiny advertisement in the *Village Voice*'s Help Wanted section, but curiosity had led her to dial the number. So here she was, one day later, preparing to sing in front of a perfect stranger for a cut of sixty bucks.

Sixty bucks might not sound like much, but when your roommate has just booted you onto your ass for failure to come through on rent—again—leaving you no place to live, and your checking account is gasping for oxygen, pink bunnies do what pink bunnies must. At least her round, fluffy tail would cushion her fall when her ass hit the sidewalk.

See? She'd already found a silver lining.

Through the eyeholes of the bunny mask, Roxy glanced down at the piece of paper in her hand. Apartment 4D. Based on the song she'd memorized on the way here and the swank interior of the building, she knew the type who would answer the door. Some too-rich, middle-aged douchebag who was so bored with his life that he needed to be entertained with novelties like singing bunny rabbits.

Roxy's gaze tracked down lower on the note in her hand, and she felt an uncomfortable kick of unease in her belly. She'd met her new boss at a tiny office in Alphabet City, surprised to find a dude only slightly older than herself running the operation. Always suspicious, she'd asked him how he kept the place afloat. There couldn't be *that* high a demand for singing telegrams, right? He'd laughed, explaining that singing bunnies only accounted for a tenth of their income. The rest came in the form of *strip-o-grams*. She'd done her best to appear flattered when he'd told her she'd be perfect for it.

She ran a thumb over the rates young-dude-boss had jotted down on the slip of paper. Two hundred dollars for each ten-minute performance. God, the *security* she would feel with that kind of money. And yet, something told her that once she took that step, once she started taking off her clothes, she would never stop. It would become a necessity instead of a temporary patch-up of her shitstorm cloud.

Think about it later. When you're not dressed like the fucking Trix Rabbit. Roxy took a deep, fortifying breath. She wrapped her steady fingers around the brass door knocker and rapped it against the wood twice. A frown marred her forehead when she heard a miserable groan come from inside the apartment. It sounded like a *young* groan. Maybe the douchebag had a son? Oh, *cool*. She definitely wanted to do this in front of someone in her age group. Perfect.

Her sarcastic thought bubble burst over her head when

the door swung open, revealing a guy. A hot-as-hell guy. A naked-except-for-unbuttoned-jeans guy. Being the shameless hussy she was, her gaze immediately dipped to his happy trail, although, on this guy, it really should have been called a rapture path. It started just beneath his belly button, which sat at the bottom of beautifully defined ab muscles. But they weren't the kind of abs honed from hours in the gym. No, they were natural, I-do-sit-ups-when-I-damn-well-feel-like-it abs. Approachable abs. The kind you could either lick or snuggle up against, depending on your mood.

Roxy lassoed her rapidly dwindling focus and yanked it higher until she met his eyes. Big mistake. The abs were child's play compared to the face. Stubbled jaw. Bed head. Big, Hershey-colored eyes outlined by dark, black lashes. His fists were planted on either side of the door frame, giving her a front-row seat to watch his chest and arms flex. A lesser woman would have applauded. As it was, Roxy was painfully aware of her bunny-costumed status, and even *that* came in second place to the fact that Approachable Abs was so stinking rich that he could afford to be nursing a hangover at eleven in the morning. On a Thursday.

He dragged a hand through his unkempt black hair. "Am I still drunk, or are you dressed like a rabbit?"

An Excerpt from

YOURS TO HOLD
Ribbon Ridge Book Two

by Darcy Burke

In the second installment of Darcy Burke's
contemporary small-town saga, the black
sheep of the Archer family is finally home,
and he's not looking for love . . . but he's about
to find it in the last place he ever expected.

Kyle Archer pulled into the large dirt lot that served as the parking area of The Alex. He still smiled when he thought of Sara coming up with the idea to name their brother's dying wish after him. It only made sense.

The hundred-plus-years-old monastery rose in front of him, its spire stretching two hundred feet into the vivid blue summer sky. The sounds of construction came from the west end of the property, down a dirt lane to what had once been a small house occupied by the head monk or whoever had been in charge at the monastery before it had been abandoned twenty-odd years ago. It was phase one of the project Alex had conceived—renovating the property into a premier hotel and event space under the Archer name, which included nine brewpubs throughout the northern valley and into Portland.

Alex had purchased the property using the trust fund left to each of them by their grandfather, then set up a trust for each sibling to inherit an equal share of the project. He'd planned for everyone to participate in the renovation, assigning key roles to all his siblings. And he'd made his attorney, Aubrey Tallinger, the trustee.

She'd endured copious amounts of anger and blame immediately following Alex's suicide because to all of them it had seemed unlikely that she'd established the trust without knowing what Alex had planned. But she insisted she hadn't known, that Alex had told her he was simply preparing in the event that he died young, something he'd convinced her was likely with his chronic lung disease.

However, things hadn't quite worked out the way Alex had envisioned. Not everyone had been eager to return to Ribbon Ridge, least of all Kyle. He shook the discomfort away. He'd fucked up. A lot. And he was trying to fix it. He owed it to Alex.

While Alex had been tethered at home with his oxygen tank and debilitating illness, the rest of them had gone off and pursued their dreams. Well, all but Hayden. As the youngest, he'd sort of gotten stuck staying in Ribbon Ridge and working for the family company. His participation in the project should've been a given, but then his dream had finally knocked down his door, and he was currently in France for a year-long internship at a winery.

Kyle stepped out of Hayden's black Honda Pilot. He'd completely taken over his brother's life while Hayden was off making wine—his car, his job, his house. Too bad Kyle couldn't also borrow the respect and appreciation Hayden received.

He slammed the car door. It wasn't going to be that easy, and he didn't deserve it to be. He should have been driving his own goddamned car, but he'd had to sell it before leaving Florida so the same shit that had driven him from Ribbon Ridge wouldn't also drive him from Miami.

But hadn't it? *No.* Things hadn't gotten as bad as they had four years ago. No one had bailed his ass out this time. He'd learned. He wasn't the same man.

An Excerpt from

THE ELUSIVE LORD EVERHART
The Rakes of Fallow Hall Series
by Vivienne Lorret

Vivienne Lorret, the *USA Today* bestselling
author of *Winning Miss Wakefield*, returns
with a new series featuring the three roguish
bachelors of Fallow Hall. Gabriel Ludlow,
Viscount Everhart, was a fool to deny the depth
of his feelings for Calliope Croft, but the threat
that kept him from her five years ago remains.
Now he must choose between two paths: break
her heart all over again or finally succumb to
loving her . . . at the risk of losing everything.

"Surely you've heard of the Chinese medicinal *massage*," Gabriel said, attempting to reassure her. Yet the low hoarseness of his voice likely sounded hungry instead. Slowly, he slid his thumbs along the outer edges of the vertebrae at the base of her neck.

"I don't believe I have," she said, relaxing marginally, her voice thin and wispy like the fine downy hairs above her nape teasing the tops of his thumbs.

"Taoist priests have used this method for centuries." His own voice came out low and insubstantial, as if he were breathing his final breath. As it was, his heart had all but given up trying to lure the blood away from his pulsing erection. *This was a terrible idea.*

He was immensely glad he'd thought of it.

His fingertips skirted the edge of her clavicle. Hands curled over her slender shoulders, he rolled his thumbs over her again.

Calliope emitted the faintest *oh*. It was barely a breath, but the sound deafened him with a rush of tumid desire. As if she sensed the change in him, she tensed again. "Are you trying to seduce me, Everhart?"

"If you have to ask," he said, attempting to add levity

with a chuckle, "then the answer is most likely *no*." Yet even he knew differently. The *most likely* was said only as a way of not lying to himself. He wanted to seduce her, slowly and for hours on end.

For five years he'd wanted to feel her flesh beneath his hands. For a moment this evening, he'd even thought this one touch would be enough to sate him. He hated being wrong.

Those pearl buttons called to him. He feathered strokes outward along the upper edges of her shoulder blades, earning another breathy sound. Only this time, she did not tense beneath the heat of his hands.

"I've read—*heard* stories," she corrected, "where the young woman is not certain of seduction until it is too late."

Gabriel caught her quick slip and was not surprised. Her penchant for reading was another aspect of her character that drew him to her. Earlier today, in fact, he'd spotted her disappearing through the library doors.

Unable to control the impulse, he'd found a servant's door off a narrow hall and surreptitiously watched her from behind a screen in the corner. Browsing the shelves, she'd searched through dozens of books. Yet her method fascinated him. She only viewed the last pages of each book. When she found one she liked, she clutched it to her breast and released a sigh filled with the type of longing he knew too well. He had little doubt that she sought the certainty of a happy ending. All in all, it had taken her over an hour to find three books that met her standards. Yet, instead of being bored, he'd been enthralled by every minute.

And now, here they were . . .

Under the spell of his massage, her head fell forward as

she arched ever-so-slightly into his hands. Rampant desire coursed through him. Even so, he was in no hurry to end this delicious torment.

"I cannot imagine that a woman would not suspect an attempt at seduction in some manner." He leaned forward to inhale the fragrance of her hair, the barest scents of rosewater and mint rising up to greet him. "Aren't all young ladies brought up with the voice of reason clamoring about in their heads?"

His gaze followed the motions of his fingers, gliding over her silken warmth, pressing against the supple flesh that pinkened under his tender ministrations. He'd always wondered . . . and now he knew she felt as soft, if not softer, than any one of his dreams.

"Curiosity has a voice as well," she said, her voice faint with pleasure. "And are we not all creatures put upon this earth to learn, just as you have learned this *exquisite* medicine?"

And sometimes curiosity could not be tamed.

It was no use. Did he truly imagine he could resist her? "Well said, Miss Croft."

Unable to hold back a moment longer, Gabriel gave in to temptation, lowered his head, and pressed his lips to her nape.